For Lora
A special friend
JR Park

The Exchange

J. R. Park

Other books by J. R. Park:

TERROR BYTE
PUNCH
UPON WAKING

Further books by the Sinister Horror Company:

THE BAD GAME – Adam Millard

CLASS THREE – Duncan P. Bradshaw
CLASS FOUR: THOSE WHO SURVIVE – Duncan P. Bradshaw
CELEBRITY CULTURE – Duncan P. Bradshaw
PRIME DIRECTIVE – Duncan P. Bradshaw

BURNING HOUSE – Daniel Marc Chant
MALDICION – Daniel Marc Chant
MR. ROBESPIERRE – Daniel Marc Chant

BITEY BACHMAN – Kayleigh Marie Edwards

GODBOMB! – Kit Power
BREAKING POINT – Kit Power

MARKED – Stuart Park

THE BLACK ROOM MANUSCRIPTS VOL 1 – Various
THE BLACK ROOM MANUSCRIPTS VOL 2 – Various

Visit JRPark.co.uk and SinisterHorrorCompany.com for further information on these and other coming titles.

THE EXCHANGE

J. R. PARK

The Exchange

First Published in 2016

Cover art by Samuel Lindup.
SamuelLindup.wordpress.com

JRPark.co.uk

ISBN: 978-0-9935926-8-3

ACKNOWLEDGEMENTS

Thanks to Stuart Park, Jorge Wiles, Dunk Bradshaw, Steph Clitheroe and Tom Dando for providing much needed feedback.

Additional thanks to Sam Lindup for the cover art, Zoe Crocker for giving me a place to write and keeping me fed, Kayleigh Ghani for forcing the unicorn issue, Steph Clitheroe (again) for the photography and encouragement, Aneta Buchwald for the translation, Dave Huggins for the beer and chat about police equipment, Thought Forms, Mugstar, Get The Blessing and Vena Cava for the inspiration, and Dan & Dunk for refusing to let me give up.

For Dunk and Dan.
You just wouldn't let it lie.
This is all your fault.

The idea for this book came to me whilst I was attending a Thought Forms album launch gig at The Exchange venue in Bristol.

As I watched the bands play I thought what a great soundtrack they would make for a movie. Within these pages you find the novelisation of the film that played in my head that night.

As I wrote the book I devised an unofficial soundtrack from the bands I'd witnessed that evening. I believe that each song in this soundtrack helps to flesh out the book's character and tone.

Boddah……………………………………Vena Cava
Black Fountain…………………………………Mugstar
OC DC…………………………………Get The Blessing
Axis Modulator…………………………………Mugstar
Ghost Mountain You And Me……………Thought Forms
Burn Me Clean……………………………Thought Forms
Industry…………………………………Thought Forms
The Unnameable……………………………Get The Blessing
Sunburnt Impendance Machine…………………Mugstar
Beyond The Sun…………………………………Mugstar
Little Ease…………………………………Get The Blessing

Where should a story start?
Exactly what is the defining moment that marks the place to begin?

Every attempt at finding a beginning will see tendrils of previous tales pulling at its circumstance, their influence shaping what is yet to be. And if we trace those back we find even more, each one a star warping each other's path with their orbits. A cosmic swirl of action and reaction that forms one perpetually moving matrix. A lattice of experience that defines our lives.

But in order to tell any tale we must pick that moment.
We must choose a beginning…

ONE

'Please don't start.'

Eleanor scowled at Jake as he continued to berate her, prematurely halting her own verbal assault before it had a chance to build momentum.

'Now isn't the time,' Jake turned back to the threatening group of people stood in front of him and placed a black briefcase on the ground at his feet.

The gold metal trim still shone even in the low light of this grey Sunday afternoon, suggesting the case to be new, but the leather was slashed and the locks dented.

Jake was six foot and thin in a way that can only be maintained by youth. His coarse, black hair blew across his face and thick rimmed glasses. Blood trickled from a cut across the bridge of his nose and dripped onto his dark green hoodie. The wound obviously fresh.

Beside him stood two friends. Eleanor was a few inches taller than Jake, her long, dark hair framed a once beautiful face, now contorted through anger and fear. Her summer dress was patterned with an intricate weave of flowers, its joyous design seeming at odds with the scene before them.

Sam stood at Jake's other side, and although he seemed dwarfed in size to his companions, his muscular frame and hardened features made him the most imposing of the three. Sam ground his teeth in anger, his jaw sliding back and forth behind a gruff, knotted beard. A crimson splash of blood coated his arms and chest although there was no sign of injury to his stocky torso. He clenched his fists as he seethed with a simmering violence.

Opposite the trio stood a woman and three men, all dressed in expensive looking business suits. Despite the cloudy day, sunglasses shielded their eyes.

Their leader, Scullin, was of equal height to Jake and stood at the forefront of his group. His muscular body filled his dark, grey suit; his mass straining against the quality wool of his jacket as he surveyed the teenagers that stood before him with an emotionless expression. The white cuff of his shirt poked out from his sleeve revealing a dark red stain.

Behind him stood King, blood was smeared down his cheeks and splattered across his light grey suit, the mess made worse from a failed attempt to wipe it off. Duell was to his right, the yellow tie that peeked out from between his pinstripe blazer matched his ruffles of blonde hair that danced in the breeze above a cold, uncaring face.

To their left was Cross. The black colour of her jacket and skirt concealed any mark that might be on them, but her tied back, blonde hair showed flecks of red dotted amongst it and a trickle of scarlet liquid ran down her thigh, pooling at the base of her stiletto heel. She pulled tightly on some rope that bound a captive girl's hands. The girl lay sobbing at Cross's feet. Her wavy brown hair stuck to her face through tears and her blue denim dress was filthy from the dusty ground.

Both groups faced each other in a moment of silence.

They stood in the centre of a building site on the edge of the city. Previously it had been a neglected wasteland; a graveyard of a more industrious age before the economic bite of recession had ripped out the jugular of commerce. But as the developed world now moved into a new period of financial growth, piles of rubble and large craters dotted the expansive area. Half-finished piping networks lay strewn next to deposits of gravel and huge holes that were dug ready for the foundations of an eagerly anticipated new retail complex. Clumps of bramble, thistle and nettle sporadically poked their way through the layers of stone, dust and dirt, making the place look like an urban desert scene.

Old buildings littered the site like a dilapidated village, ready to be knocked down. Damp, rot and the elements had laid their withering claim, caving roofs in, turning up floors and driving cracks into the walls. These structures had died years ago, only remnants of their shells remained, waiting to be destroyed.

Of late this place had been a hive of activity. A crew of workman arrived every day to complete the demolition and new construction. But today it remained quiet, free of hard hats and high-vis jackets. Today the workforce remained at home enjoying Sunday pursuits of their own leisure, leaving the place steeped in a brooding silence.

Muted sounds of far off city traffic drifted through the air. Gently building winds whipped across the site as the sky throbbed in an unsettled grey, waiting for something to happen.

'You came without guns?' Jake called out to Scullin, breaking the silence.

'As promised,' Scullin replied, holding his monstrously large palms out to show they were empty. 'You made your threat very succinctly.'

'That's right. Our man's hidden; watching you,' he restated the threat in an attempt to reassure himself. His cheek throbbed, a reminder of the hard knuckles possessed by his opponent. 'If there's any funny business he'll make a phone call and have this place swarming with cops.'

The threat was empty. He knew if the cops came they'd make a run for it, disappearing and taking Laura with them. If that happened he might never see his girlfriend again. He prayed they didn't see through his bluff.

Eleanor bored angry eyes into the back of Jake's skull, still feeling some resentment over the argument they'd had whilst walking to the agreed meeting place. She was furious they had gotten into this situation, but deep down she knew he was right, this was not a time to be fighting amongst themselves. They could work out where the blame lay once they got out of this.

If they got out of this.

'There's the case,' Jake pointed to the battered item at his feet.

Scullin looked at it with a quizzical expression.

'You were expecting more?' Sam snorted.

'Sam, don't,' Eleanor placed her long, slender fingers tenderly but nervously on his shoulder in an attempt to calm him.

The red stains across Sam's body were testament to the lack of limits his aggression knew. Despite his earlier heroic act to save them, he worried her. Eleanor's stomach tightened as she thought back to the sickening atrocity she had witnessed in one of the crumbling buildings, but was glad to feel Sam relax slightly; easing his shoulder into her gentle touch, even though his brow stayed furrowed.

Both groups continued to eye each other with a patient intensity.

Subtly breaking the stand-off, Cross smiled with vicious delight as she dug her long nails into the skin of the girl that lay at her feet. The light wind stifled the cries of her hapless victim as Cross's blue painted talons sunk into the soft flesh of the girl's wrists.

'Laura!' Jake turned to the distraught girl, 'I'm so sorry, Laura. We didn't mean to leave you honey, we didn't mean-'

'I can't believe you, Jake,' Laura wailed. 'I can't believe you did this.'

Jake tried to continue but his words broke down to barely suppressed sobs of regret, mirroring those of his girlfriend. Scullin's contemptuous laugh cut through the boy's weak pleas for forgiveness.

'How quickly the bonds of love can unravel when

faced with death,' Scullin's voice felt as rough as gravel as it echoed through Jake's body, yet it managed to hold a tonal quality that provided an edge of soothing eloquence. The almost impossible juxtaposition made the young man shudder as he listened to every syllable. 'You're so young. You know nothing. You have yet to truly understand what really holds everything together.'

'Shut your fucking mouth,' Sam called out, scratching his beard in irritation and begging for a fight. 'It's a little dark for sunglasses ain't it? Did you lot leave your guide dogs at home?'

'These sunglasses are for your protection,' Scullin answered back with a smile. His voice remained calm, at odds with the threat in his words. 'You don't want to see my eyes. There's so much rage in them right now you'll shit your pants like the little boy you are.'

Sam broke from Eleanor's soft grip and motioned forward, enraged by this insult but glad of the justification. Cross reacted by pulling Laura closer to her, tightening the ropes around her wrists and digging her nails in again. Laura squealed in pain. Jake put his hand out signalling his friend to stop. Sam reluctantly obeyed, growling under his breath.

'We can take them,' Sam muttered so as only audible to Jake.

'We can't take the chance,' his friend replied. 'We're lucky Laura's still alive. I'm not rolling the dice a second time.'

Sam started to argue back but their private conversation was cut short by an unnerving voice that sliced through the strengthening winds.

'You've caused us a great deal of trouble,' Scullin

bellowed before turning to his blood splattered colleague in the light grey suit. 'King, check the case,' he ordered.

They were pushing the boundaries. Testing the threats.

'Not so fast,' Jake replied, causing King to halt his progress. A sliver of courage returned to Jake's tone, beating back the panic of a ruse unravelled. 'Give us the girl.' He squeezed his fists and pointed angrily at Scullin, 'Give me back Laura.'

'Oh really?' mocked Scullin. 'And what are you going to do? Are you going to stop us?'

Jake narrowed his eyes and, without breaking gaze with the man stood opposite, kicked the briefcase. It fell on its side and in doing so swung a chain round that was attached to the handle. The metallic links flew through the air in an arc before crashing into the dusty earth, revealing the end to be wrapped around the freshly mutilated remains of a severed hand. Its wrist grotesquely ended with a ragged and bloody stump, still dribbling claret liquid from the recent dismemberment.

'Don't forget,' Jake threatened through clenched teeth, 'we've still got one of your men.'

TWO

Hidden in the darkness, inside the basement of one of the derelict buildings a man sat, slumped forward on a battered, old chair. The ropes that bound him ran tightly round his torso, crushing creases into his wool suit. Muted daylight tinted by the coming storm penetrated the cracks in the ceiling but was quickly engulfed by the blackness that surrounded the unconscious prisoner. His dark silhouette sunk forward whilst blood dripped from his head, running off the sunglasses on his face and forming tiny rivulets on the floor. His arms were tied behind his back whilst more blood poured from the sleeve of his left arm. A gory stump protruded from his suit jacket, dangling pieces of mangled flesh and torn skin where his hand should be. By his feet lay the remains of a hacksaw blade, snapped from its frame and discarded after the pressures of its grisly work.

Knight slowly regained consciousness as he remained prisoner, tied to the long neglected piece of furniture, left over from a time when this was a busy office. His one remaining hand felt the cold, rusted pole of the chair leg and he squeezed it as he collected his thoughts. Gently his fingers searched out for his horrific wound and carefully he prodded the end of his arm, probing the flesh to understand the extent of his injury. In the distance he heard a noise, the faint sound of voices, and without raising his head he broke into a smile.

'Come on,' Ollie cursed his phone as he checked the display then waved it in the air.

He placed it against his ear to find the same result as before: silence. He swung against the frame as he hung in the doorway of one of the disused buildings, his long, black hair catching in his beard as he talked out loud.

'Nothing, just nothing,' he protested. 'It's connecting then loses signal again. Like it's coming in waves. Bloody network. There's no calling the cops if this goes all wrong. So much for Plan B.'

He put the phone back in his pocket and kicked the crumbling doorway in frustration. Small rocks fell from the stonework, dislodged by the impact. Idly scratching the tattoo that trailed up his arm, an abstract portrait of Marilyn Munroe, Ollie turned his back on the old construction and looked across the desolate building site. He'd never appreciated the size of this wasteland before. He'd ridden past it many times on his bike, but only now, stood in the confines of the security fence, did he realise just how vast it was.

Across the other side of the site he could see the

hole in the fence where they had made their accidental entrance, and a short distance beyond was Sam's smashed up van. They had hit the fence with some force when the driver lost control. Luckily it managed to punch a hole straight through the steel links, but had left the van unusable. The lights were smashed, the front grill buckled and the white paint was scratched by the torn fencing, leaving a silver scarring etched along the bodywork. Not that it would have lasted much longer anyway. The vehicle was already dying before they'd crashed into the perimeter of the *yet to be* Oracle shopping centre. Ollie scanned his eyes across the ravished bodywork, making out six bullet holes. It had felt like more when they were inside the vehicle making their getaway, but that didn't include the ones that hit the tyres. They had felt the tyres blow at eighty miles per hour and now the only evidence of their existence were scraps of shredded rubber clinging to the buckled, asymmetrical wheels. The petrol tank had also been hit and the flammable liquid was still draining out underneath the pitiful wreck. It was those kind of expert crack shots from the lot in suits that had forced them to ditch their vehicle and seek shelter.

Even when the tyres were shot out, Sam had wrestled with the van through the busy traffic. He'd managed to give them the slip as he took chances through lights and busy lanes, but as metal rims wore onto the tarmac he lost control and crashed. Their pursuers eventually caught up, but at least it had given them time to hide.

Not that hiding had done them much good.

'When we get out of this, Sam is going to lose his

shit over his van,' Ollie remarked with a mixture of amusement and disbelief.

The van was used in Sam's trade as a builder and the ride had been uncomfortable as they had dived into the back, forcing Ollie to lie on a bag of tools. But at the time comfort was not a consideration, only survival was.

Ollie pressed his bruised thigh. It stung at the point where he had landed on an exposed drill bit. He hadn't felt it at the time, adrenalin acting as a powerful pain suppressant, but as its effects drained away, the pain began to grow.

Leaving the bruise to throb, he rubbed his head and pondered.

Sam was a builder but Ollie knew him for his other vocation; that of obtaining and dealing the best weed west of the city. Sam moved in shadowy worlds as he scored his sought after contraband, but Ollie had never seen such an outburst from the stocky muscleman. Maybe it was because Sam had been so angry about his vehicle, but even that was no excuse to what Ollie had just witnessed. He shuddered as he recalled it. He knew never to cross his friend, but *that* was just insane. It didn't matter whether he scored the best marijuana or not, Sam was not a man Ollie wanted to get mixed up with any more.

But if it wasn't for his crazy friend calling out in his van and making a getaway they might have all been goners anyway. Confused by his own reasoning he abandoned this line of thinking and refocused on the present.

Ollie turned his attention across the wasteland. In the distance he could see Jake, Sam and Eleanor. They had arrived at the meeting point with the briefcase as planned. Straining his eyes he could just make out Laura slumped to the floor beneath one of their pursuers.

If they hadn't accidentally left Laura in the clutches of the others they all could have walked away from this; dumped the case and just ran.

I hope she's alright, he thought. *That bitch with blonde hair looked pretty mean, but,* he confessed, *kind of hot. Better than the other…*

'Hang on a minute,' Ollie muttered, beginning to vocalise his thoughts, 'wasn't there another woman? Hey Kayleigh,' he shouted back into the building, 'weren't there two women with that lot? Kayleigh? Kayleigh!'

Ollie's voice echoed down the corridor, but by the time it reached Kayleigh's ears it had lost all recognisable form. It was as if the darkness had swallowed the sound. She squeezed the charm in her pocket tightly for courage as she shuffled forward through the swirling blackness of the abandoned building. With no electricity to light the way her surroundings grew darker the deeper she went. The lack of light caused no problems though, she knew where she was going; retracing the steps she had taken only a few moments earlier.

Kayleigh had been thankful to leave the basement before, pushing past her friends to vacate the scene of torture and brutality. But as they stood in the doorway watching Sam and Eleanor walk off to meet Jake with the briefcase and make the exchange, her mind had drifted back to the man in the darkness. She felt something silently call her, willing her to make the pitch black journey down the staircase to where the wretched man sat, trussed up and bleeding.

Edging her feet against the end of each step and lowering herself gently, Kayleigh carefully made her way down the stairs, back to the basement where moments earlier they'd been hiding like scared animals, trying to make sense of what had happened.

Even now she didn't have a clue.

Her thoughts had been a collage of confusion since she'd woken up this morning. Despite the crazy events and situations this Sunday afternoon had brought her, Kayleigh had been unable to shake the dream she'd woken from with such a terrible fright. Despite the gun shots, despite the car chase, despite the death threats, the dream refused to leave her.

As she approached the bottom of the stairs, the sound of water droplets echoed unseen in the subterranean level. Kayleigh placed her hands against the cold, damp wall and peeked round the corner, spying on their wounded hostage. Her stomach grew light, feeling like it was crawling round her body, desperate to climb up her throat and out through her mouth. An attempt to swallow only resulted in an involuntary shiver.

Her ears rang with a shrill whine against the eerie calm. Unknown whispers seemed to call behind the high-pitched frequency, both their origins and meaning lost to their audible subtlety.

She thought back to her plagued sleep. The deathly vision that had seeped through the blackness of her unconscious. Those piercing, hellish eyes.

She gripped her stomach and held her breath.

Knight lifted his head and, without turning to face her, spoke softly.

'Hello my dear,' he said, 'you have something of mine.'

Kayleigh stepped forward, and through the inky atmosphere her image, washed of colour, fell into his view. The metallic frame of her glasses glinted from the slivers of light that somehow managed to weakly filter into these depths. Her long, straight hair rested gently on her shoulders and hung just past her breasts. Her face was one of concern and worry.

'I'm sorry,' she spoke with sincerity, 'we didn't want this.'

'What did you want?' Knight asked.

'I don't know. Not this! We have no control over Sam,' Kayleigh stepped back, suddenly wary of her prisoner, 'he's a psycho. I had no idea he was going to cut your hand off. Fucking hell, that's your hand…'

A tear fell gently down her cheek. Knight seemed unmoved by this display of compassion.

'We tried to stop him,' she continued, 'but he's so big. He's so scary. If you'd have been conscious you would have seen us trying to stop him.'

'He wants the case,' Knight spoke matter-of-factly.

'But he doesn't even know what's in it.'

'That matters little to Sam. He feels the pull, the desire. He senses the power. People do scary things for the contents of that case. Very scary things.' He turned his head to face her. 'Are you scared now, Kayleigh?'

'How do you know my name?' Kayleigh sounded startled, surprised by the knowledge of this apparent stranger.

She thought back to her dream. Those horrid eyes. The pain in her stomach. The blood draining from her body.

Her nightmarish vision began to spread through her thoughts, uncontrolled and untamed. Fragmented memories of her dream began to expand, filling in the gaps that her sudden waking this morning had left, clouding the girl's mind with dread and horror.

'I know many things, Kayleigh. Things you wouldn't even dare to imagine. I know your name. I know where you live. I know you hold yourself back and refuse to let go.'

Knight smiled as the girl edged backwards in the gloom.

'I know what you dreamt last night.'

THREE

'Only an imbecile would dare stand in our way,' Scullin remarked in a chillingly flat tone.

Jake looked on, holding his ground and trying desperately to keep his nerve.

Overhead the grey clouds grew darker, their presence heavy in the sky as they congregated above the ground where the two groups stood. A distant rumble of thunder felt its way through the claustrophobic summer air, like a growling beast warning of its hostile nature.

'What's in the case?' Sam snarled through his bushy, red beard.

Eleanor stood pensively behind him, chewing her nails with worry.

'You've tried to open it,' Scullin eyed the briefcase that stood between them, its battered and scratched outer clearly displayed their attempts at an enforced entry. 'No luck I see. Hardly a surprise.'

The heavy chain secured to the case had coiled on the floor beside it. The grisly contents at the other end of the heavy-duty links nestled in the centre of the circular pattern. Knight's severed hand was ghostly white, the blood long since drained from the hacked flesh of its barbaric amputation. Loose tendrils of skin trailed from the mangled wrist and flapped in the growing wind like rags on a washing line.

Jake looked towards Laura as she lay at Cross's feet. The vicious, blood-soaked woman grinned maliciously behind her sunglasses, causing Jake's mouth to dry.

'What's in it?' Sam barked again, his temper beginning to flare once more.

'Nothing for your eyes,' Scullin scoffed. 'But you want it don't you? You want its secrets. I know you can feel it, Sam. You can feel its power.'

'How do you know my name?' Sam bellowed, thumping his chest in a sign of aggression, angry that he identified with the other man's words. He glanced at the case between them and heard its contents silently call. 'You'd better open up that briefcase,' he threatened Scullin.

'It seems were at a deadlock. The case is before us, but sealed shut. The key you stole from Knight is useless without its counterpart. In turn, the one I possess will be nothing without the other. So return to me what you stole,' Scullin commanded. 'Give me back the key.'

'Guys?' Jake turned to his friends, confused by the demand.

Sam and Eleanor's blank faces mirrored his. They hadn't seen a key.

Duell stepped towards Scullin, weary of this exchange. 'We don't need to put up with this,' he whispered to his leader in an irritated tone. 'Let's just take them out. There must be another way to find Knight and flush out the-'

'We don't have your key,' Jake said turning back. 'I don't want any tricks. I want to play this straight. You take the case, we take the girl. We tell you where your friend's hidden and we'll all walk away. Deal?'

Scullin clenched his jaw, his sunglasses masking his reaction as he silently regarded the eighteen year old that stood in front of him. Jake's last words hung in the air, their authority dissolving in the proceeding silence.

'Lies. If I give you the girl, what means do I have of holding you to your end of the bargain? I'd be a fool to give her up so easily,' Scullin rasped through gritted teeth, eventually breaking the quiet. 'Take us to Knight.'

Spurred on by the outburst, Cross leant forward and took hold of her prisoner. Laura tried her best not to cry out as Cross gripped her neck, but as her tormentor's fingernails broke her skin the pain proved too much. Blood trickled from the wounds and down her nape, soaking into her blue, denim dress.

'You bitch,' Laura cursed in protest, gasping for air.

Cross continued to squeeze, choking her victim whilst all the while watching Jake and his companions with an evil intensity that begged them to come at her.

'Oh come on, little boy,' she mocked, watching Jake grow angry, powerless to stop the torture. 'Please, try it.'

Laura's face grew red as she thrashed around in Cross's hold, growing weaker by the second. Her cheeks turning a shade of purple before she was released from the grip and thrown to the floor. She gasped wildly for air and held her bruised throat.

'Why are we playing these games?' Duell muttered

to himself.

Taking a handful of Laura's hair, Cross pulled her hostage back onto her knees. Tilting the poor girl's head forward she clawed at her exposed neck, raking Laura's flesh and tearing four savage wounds that instantly filled with dark, red blood.

'Stop this!' Eleanor shouted, halting Sam in his tracks before he had a chance to charge forward.

She was a naturally nervous girl without a drink in her hand, but the suffering of her best friend forced an outburst. The two had been inseparable since the age of five, and although leaving her behind earlier had been an accident, it still caused guilt to gnaw away at Eleanor's insides.

'Leave her alone! She hasn't done anything,' Eleanor continued, trying to talk some sense into the situation. 'Let's make the trade and-'

Laura screamed as Cross squeezed the girl's neck, forcing blood to pump from her wounds.

'I thought you loved me, Jake,' the captive girl cried as Cross gleefully licked the teenager's blood from her fingers. 'Ellie, why did you leave me? Please, make them stop.'

Cross raised her hand behind her head once more, preparing to slash her blood drenched talons across the girl's cheek, as she turned Laura to face her. The nineteen year old stared wide-eyed, unable to break free from her tormentor's powerful grip.

'We cut your man's hand off,' desperation peppered Jake's words. Abhorred, as he had been by Sam's previously crazed attack, he now used it as a weapon; some leverage in bargaining for Laura's safety. 'We've done as you said. As you called out. We came out of hiding and brought the briefcase. Make the exchange and we'll tell you where you can find your friend.' Jake raised his fist in anger, stifling tears that collected behind his eyes. He shouted as he tried to mask his wavering nerves. 'We'll do a lot more to him if you don't hand back the girl.'

'What about the key?' Scullin demanded.

'Jake…' Laura called feebly, terrified as Cross's arm poised with the menace of a coiled cobra.

'My friends have it!' Jake blurted out. It was a lie, but as Cross threw Laura to the ground and turned her attention back to the group, it had the outcome he'd desired.

'And where are *they*?' Scullin's words took on a new intensity.

'Not until you hand back the girl,' said Jake, standing his ground.

Duell grabbed his leader's arm, just above the elbow and gently squeezed it, attracting his attention. 'We can take them,' his frustration spoken in hushed tones so only Scullin could hear. 'Why are we playing around? Fuck Knight, he's bleeding to death anyway. Let him die.'

Scullin flexed his bicep, expanding its size enough to break Duell's grip.

'If we lose that key we'll never get the case open in time,' Scullin spoke with a calm that was nearing the limits of its patience. 'We can't miss this chance. Everything has fallen into place.'

'But-' Duell tried to respond.

'He's right,' King interrupted. 'It's of no

coincidence the opportunity presented itself to us at the time of the Calling. We've been so careful to execute our plan. And maybe this is some kind of test. But we can't miss this window. We need that key.'

'Tell me, Jake,' Scullin began, refocusing his attention, 'earlier today, before our unfortunate encounter, did you turn back and look at the police officer that was chasing you? Did you get a good look at their face?'

Confused, Jake's mind tried its best to reach back in time, to remember the chase with the authorities earlier this morning.

Scullin laughed to see his reaction. 'Of course, you're not used to seeing her in uniform, are you? She's so new to the force.'

Jake's complexion grew paler as the words sunk in.

'Please,' Scullin turned to Duell, 'go to the car and retrieve our guest in blue.'

'My pleasure,' Duell replied, his voice as steely-cold as his chiselled expression.

Turning around and heading away from the group, the faintest trace of a smile plagued the corners of his mouth.

'No. You didn't… You can't…' Jake struggled to find speech as his thoughts flooded with abhorrent possibilities.

'Oh, we haven't hurt her… *yet.* At least, not much.' Shades of sadistic pleasure resonated through Scullin's voice. 'You will tell us where you have Knight, and where you've hidden the key, otherwise you'll be watching Special Constable Forrest draw her last, agonising breath.'

'No…' Jake's voice faded, swallowed up by the wind.

'If you don't cooperate you'd best prepare to say goodbye, Jake *Forrest*. Say goodbye to your sister.'

FOUR

Through tinted glass the storm looked even more threatening as the foreboding darkness deepened. Special Constable Aimee Forrest slowly regained consciousness; as she did so her eyes fell on the view through the darkened window of a limousine. In the distance a group of figures stood in two opposing groups amidst the barren landscape of a sprawling building site. Still dazed, she sat upright in the back of the luxury car, igniting fires of agony through her body. Her head throbbed as she felt the warm, wet tenderness of her wounded temple.

Her thoughts slewed together as she tried to make sense of her surroundings, fighting through a fog of semi-consciousness and pain.

The interior of the limousine was a hazy patchwork of white and red, but as her eyes began to focus she soon realised the strawberry and cream décor was something far more sinister. Her fingers reached out and touched the red pattern, smearing it across the white background. It stuck to her fingers and wafted a metallic smell, stimulating her nostrils to flare at the familiar, but unwelcome odour. Looking round she saw the same red, splattered throughout the inside of the vehicle, from the floor to the ceiling, and smeared across the tinted windows.

The blood was fresh.

Outside she could see the shape of another vehicle. A black Audi A5 stood motionless and seemingly unoccupied.

Turning around she caught sight of something crumpled in the furthest corner of the limousine. Its limbs bent at awkward angles over the leather interior.

Aimee held her breath as the memories came flooding back.

'Osborne,' she whispered, scared of making too loud a sound.

She slid beside her colleague as he lay, sprawled out on the back seat, his uniform soaked to an even darker shade as a growing pool of crimson surrounded his broken body.

'Osborne,' she whispered again, quietly but firmly.

Fearing the worst, Aimee placed her hands against his throat, sighing deeply with relief when she felt a pulse. It was weak but he was still alive. Forcing his vest up, she searched for the source of the bleeding and located three ragged holes across his stomach. Remembering her training she straightened her fingers and plunged them deep inside the bloody openings.

PC Osborne's eyes shot open as the pain of her gruesome first aid surged through his body. His shoulders shook and his eyes rolled wildly as she pushed into his tender flesh. Pathetically he flailed like the protests of a rag doll, until at last he focused on the Special Constable with a look of recognition and a quietening sense of calm.

'Forrest…' a weak whisper was all he could muster. 'A bit of a shitter for your second day out, huh?'

He gave a faint smile of reassurance, flashing a chipped tooth and failing to mask the agony across his face. Aimee tried to force a smile back, to comfort her wounded colleague, but her cheeks only contorted with sadness. She felt blood dribble from his wounds, run along her fingers and trickle down her arm.

'This is horrible,' she replied trying to fight back tears whilst pushing her digits deeper into his injuries in an attempt to plug the holes and stem the bleeding.

'You're doing… good, kid,' Osborne gurgled his speech as blood filled his throat. 'Just like we taught you in training.'

'I had a good teacher,' she spoke through gritted teeth.

'Forrest… ' Osborne tried to touch her face but lacked the strength to reach her.

'Don't try to move,' Aimee instructed. 'We'll get through this.'

'Aimee…' he struggled with his words. 'You can't save me. I've already lost too much blood. I thought I'd be dead already.' He gently smiled, 'I guess God is looking favourably on me today. Giving me a few extra minutes to look on your pretty face.'

She felt tears well up behind her eyes.

'You're not going to die,' she said, angrily fighting back the desire to cry.

'It's too late for me,' he continued. 'You've got to help those kids.'

The Police Constable's skin grew paler as he tried to stifle a groan of pain.

Aimee glanced out the limousine window and clocked the group in the centre of the building site. A dark figure, dressed in a suit, was making its way up the hill towards the car.

She looked towards the Audi; it remained still.

'I can't do this alone,' Aimee protested, turning back to her colleague. 'I'm just a Special. A part time cop. I wouldn't have even passed training if it wasn't for you!'

'Forrest, you *can* do this,' Osborne retorted.

'I can't.'

'Yes you can. You have to. They need you. Call for back up. Get some help.' He paused to swallow the blood collecting in his mouth. 'They're little scum bags… but they don't deserve to die.'

'Neither do you,' tears trickled gently down her cheeks. 'I'm so sorry.'

Quickly looking out the window again she saw the figure getting closer, rapidly covering the distance between them.

'It's not your fault. We didn't stand a chance.' His voice weakened and his eyes began to drift, losing focus on her and meandering towards the blood splattered ceiling. 'Save those kids for me, especially that damn brother of yours. . .'

'Andy,' she shouted.

PC Andrew Osborne's features relaxed as all the muscles in his face let go. His body fell limp and his head rolled on his neck, resting against his chest.

Vacant eyes stared from a blank face, an expressionless visage. Even his smile had faded in death, leaving an empty hollowness.

Special Constable Forrest shuddered at the sight, giving herself to the grief she'd been stifling.

'No, no, no, no!' she screamed in anger, punching the seat.

Aimee pulled her gore covered fingers from Osborne's wounds and watched a torrent of dark red liquid pour from his injuries, spilling onto the carpeted floor.

The figure loomed large outside, like the shadow of death ready to take Osborne from this world. It was so close she could make out the sound of stones crunching under its steps.

Aimee reached for her radio, but couldn't find it clipped to her vest. Patting herself down and scanning the inside of the car confirmed it was not close by.

Shit! Those bastards must have taken it, she thought to herself.

Why didn't she use the radio earlier? She should have used it the moment she'd heard gunshots in the street. She should have pressed its panic button, sending a signal back to control and alerting them of their location.

But she'd froze, whilst everything else around her sped up. Everything happened so fast…

Shit!

Part time cop she may be, but she needed to get herself, and those idiot kids, out of this situation and to safety. Whoever that lot in suits were, it was clear they knew what they were doing, and they were deadly.

Aimee grasped the door handle of the limousine, but found the door locked. Trying the other side she found the same. Trapped but undeterred, the Special Constable rolled onto her back and raised her knees to her chest. Kicking out, she landed her heavy boots squarely in the centre of the glass. The tinted window hardly even shook as pain shot up Aimee's already bruised thighs. No doubt this was reinforced glass. Sledge hammers couldn't get through this stuff. As athletic and stubborn as she was, Aimee had no chance of breaking it.

Helplessly watching through the window she saw the figure approach. At only fifty metres away she could see the blank expression on his face. Like that of Osborne's. Like that of death.

She had to get out.

She had to get help.

Desperately, Aimee searched through the limousine, looking for anything that could aid her. Did they leave a gun behind; a key? The last few hours had been a sea of panic and it seemed all sides had struggled to stay afloat as they were swept along by each other's currents.

Mistakes could easily be made.

But not with these guys it seemed.

The inside of the car was empty, devoid of anything except the seats, not even a pen or a loose button.

Devoid of anything, that was, except for her and PC Osborne.

As she approached him she tried to fight off her swelling feelings of grief. His skin was rapidly growing cold and felt unreal to her touch as she searched his body. He had already been stripped of everything useful by their abductors, except for one thing.

Those bastards had been careful, meticulously professional, but had made one mistake.

As broken as it was, shattered by the impact of a bullet, the remnants of a police radio hung from his vest, nestled in the shadows of the seat.

Picking it up, Aimee cradled the radio, wiping it clear of blood and examining the contraption. The casing had splintered into pieces and was tenuously held together by strands of wire and solder. The battery pack however, was still intact and carefully she was able to reconnect the loose wires, re-establishing power. The radio burst into life with an ear bludgeoning wave of static. The speaker crackled and hissed a torrent of interference as Aimee tried to pick up a clear signal. Voices floated in and out of the white noise, but only for a few tantalising moments before being lost to the howls of feedback and the melee of sounds.

The figure outside filled the window; his image grew taller the closer he got. The blank expression on his face looked ghostly with its emotionless stare, but there was deadly threat in the curled corners of his mouth; an unsavoury anticipation.

Aimee gripped the radio and held it close, hoping it would work and delirious with the possibility of rescue. Unsure of its capability, she jabbed at the panic button before speaking into the receiver.

'Hello? Hello?' All of Aimee's training had been wiped from her mind in her panicked state. 'Hello? This is Special Constable Forrest. I've been kidnapped and held hostage on the new Oracle Centre construction site. PC Osborne has been killed.' She began to shout, trying to fight through the noise, 'And we have a number of civilians under threat from an armed but unknown group.' Franticly, Aimee tried to think of the correct protocol, the terms she had practised many times over, but nothing came to mind.

The approaching man was only metres away.

Aimee looked at the group of kids in the distance, in over their heads, then caught sight of herself in the rear view mirror. A frightened twenty-five year old trembled back at her. Osborne was wrong, she couldn't handle this. She was no cop.

'Please help us,' she cried, praying someone would hear her call. 'Anyone, please help us.'

FIVE

Of all the dreams and visions Taal had been subjected to since their journey began, none had been as vivid and haunting as this one. It was as if all of creation had stopped still, frozen in microcosm before his eyes; a picture postcard of eternity that hung from invisible hooks in all its terrifying beauty.

The vision had only been fleeting, but it told him enough. It told him they were on the right path and were getting closer.

He was thankful for its brevity.

Even with his years of experience and training, Taal was unsure just how long his body and mind could have coped with such a sight. His gnarled, worn hands gripped his wooden staff, and although his face showed no signs of emotion, inwardly he smiled; thankful that his companions had not been subjected to the forces that they currently followed.

It was dark inside the trailer as the lorry rumbled along the motorway. So dark that Taal could barely make out his faithful companions as they sat patiently, stowed away from the prying eyes of the border control, awaiting for the next command from their leader.

Exactly how old Taal was, no one was sure. In appearance he looked deceptively thin and frail, as if his whole body had been pulled tightly around his bones. His skin was a light brown colour, tough and weathered like old leather. The robes that covered his body seemed oversized, engulfing his small frame and tiny stature. The material was grey in colour with flashes of gold and blue wound into simplistic but carefully measured patterns. Similar markings were painted onto his face and continued over his large, hairless head. His features held an expression of ever present calm whilst his eyes held a glint from centuries of wisdom.

His travelling companions made for a strange menagerie of the human race, but such was the way with the Servants of the Sacred Whisper. It did not discriminate with those it called.

Sanay was a strong man, probably in his early thirties. He spoke with a Germanic accent and always had a smile beneath those crisp, sky-like eyes. Maja was maybe a decade younger than him. Her thick, black hair was wrapped in a headdress, whose gold patterns twinkled like stars as she moved, even in the darkness. Her Polish accent had softened over time, but still reverberated through her words when she spoke. How such a young girl heard the whisper on the winds and made her way to the temple was a story untold, although such an early calling had marked her as a talent to be watchful for.

No one spoke of the lives they'd had before they

entered the pact of the Servitude. It was irrelevant. Histories would be abandoned, families forgotten, names changed.

No one asked.

No one cared.

Kal, their fourth companion, carried large, thick scars across his face. Mementos from a hideous act of violence that had left his midnight-black skin permanently marked and forever foul to the human eye. Where he came from and what had happened was never queried. Kal had found his way across the continents, following the words in the breeze, and entered the temple. Like all seekers, he was relieved to find he wasn't alone, discovering his seeming madness was a gift shared by others.

Taal recalled each of their rebirths. Everyone he'd witnessed first-hand. But despite his superior level within the Servitude he felt it an honour to be partnered on this journey with such esteemed company. He knew of their potential and the role they would play, even though it hadn't been made fully clear to them yet. All secrets would be revealed in time.

The vibrations in the lorry softened until they felt the vehicle slow to a stop. Taal looked up from his meditations. It had been a long and arduous passage, and whilst they had encountered kindness on their journey, they had also borne the brunt of abhorrent cruelty. Their destination was still some distance away and he sensed more adversity before they reached their goal.

Muffled voices outside the stationary lorry caught all their ears.

'What can I help you with, officer?' Taal recognised the voice of the driver.

'What's your business?' another voice replied, sneering his words.

The Servitude remained seated in the dark. They looked to Taal for guidance. He did not move, but carefully listened.

'Transporting this load up to Newcastle,' the driver answered. 'Been on the road most of the day. Came in over the Channel and straight up the motorway. Still a journey ahead of me.'

'Newcastle, huh? And what is this a load of?' his questioner sounded suspicious.

'Uh…brake pads. Seventeen thousand brake pads. We all gotta stop sometime.' He laughed nervously but was met with a steely silence.

The trailer echoed as the man outside tapped against its metal hull.

'Are you aware you've been leaking fluid for the last few miles?' the muffled voice of the officer grew more agitated. 'Didn't you do your walk round checks before you set off?'

'Leaking? Really? It was fine when I left,' the driver defended himself.

'Open this trailer up,' a new voice called out. 'Let's see these brake pads.'

'I've really got to be heading on, I'm behind schedule as it is,' the driver's feeble tone wavered, matching his fading conviction.

'Just get it open.'

A heavy clunk thudded against the steel walls, then slowly the doors of the trailer began to open. Light crept in from the outside, illuminating the four robed passengers. They rose to their feet blinking at the three silhouettes that stood on the roadside peering in.

'What have we here?' a booming voice called out. 'Come on you lot, out of there. Slowly.'

As the eyes of the uncovered passengers grew accustomed to the light, the silhouettes outside became more detailed, revealing a worried truck driver and two large policemen. Taal, Maja, Sanay and Kal obediently made their way out of the lorry and knelt down by the roadside.

'You have been a prize wally,' the policeman with the thick, black moustache dryly remarked to the driver. 'Smuggling immigrants into the country? Not a wise move.'

The policeman took hold of the driver and pushed him into the side panel of the lorry, slamming his face against the metal that displayed the logo of a car company. His lip split on the impact and blood dribbled down his chin.

'Steady Byrne,' the policeman's colleague called out.

'Can it, Wallis,' Byrne called back, taking the driver's hands behind his back and aggressively forcing a pair of handcuffs onto his wrists.

The driver winced in pain.

Pleased with his work, Byrne turned his attention to the four bizarrely dressed stowaways.

'Where on earth are you lot from? Have you escaped some travelling circus?' he laughed as he slowly walked closer to the line-up in order to take a better look.

They remained silent, watching him with attentive

concentration.

'What's the matter? You don't speak? Oh come on, you can talk to little ole me, I won't bite,' his words dripped with insincerity.

Again his comments were met with a mute reaction.

'Who are you?' he seethed.

Still his question went unanswered.

Byrne's face grew red as his simmering rage boiled over.

'FUCKING ANSWER ME!' he screamed directly into the face of Taal.

Taal's facial expression did not change, remaining calm and neutral. This only enraged the police officer further.

'So you're not going to talk?' his tone retreated to a sinister serenity. 'You're not going to tell me who you are or why you're hiding out in this lorry? Really? That's how you want to play it? Damn, you are going to be in so much trouble.' Byrne gave a malicious grin.

He seemed to be getting off on this exchange, revelling in the confrontation and the power. Taal noticed a swelling in the policeman's trousers.

'What's with these stupid outfits?' he continued, prodding their grey robes. 'What the fuck are you wearing? And what happened to you, boy? What's with this scar shit all over your face?'

Byrne stopped in front of Kal and grabbed his shoulders with both hands. He gripped hard and pulled Kal to his feet, bringing their eyes level.

'Kal!' Maja called out, concerned for her companion and rising to defend him.

Sanay took hold of her and pulled her back to her knees.

Taal remained still, watching the foray unfold before him.

'Kal, hey?' Byrne spat his words. 'What are you doing, Kal?' He shook him wildly whilst he bellowed into Kal's distressed expression. 'You fucking scarred freak! Is this some kind of terrorist thing? What are you? Some bunch of religious nuts come to blow us up? Or are you even lower than that? Are you just some pissant refugees? Sneaking your way into this country so you can scrounge off the state whilst the likes of me and Wallis foot the bill through our taxes. I'd rather have you pull a gun. At least then I take care of you quickly. Might even earn myself a commendation.'

'Come on Byrne, leave it out,' Wallis said placing a calming hand on his colleague's shoulder.

'Get that fucking driver in the back of the fucking car,' Byrne replied, barking his orders through gritted teeth whilst all the while maintaining eye contact with Kal. 'Radio through to the station and tell them what we've got. That truck needs to be impounded.'

Wallis acquiesced to this order. He knew what was going to happen next, he'd seen it countless times before. It wasn't the first time he'd had to cover for his partner's violent streaks, and it wouldn't be the last. It was morally hard to swallow, but it was the price he paid for a quiet life in the force. Wallis led the obese driver to the car, and as he explained his arrest he heard the sickening slap of knuckle against cheek.

Kal landed in a crumpled heap on the floor, bleeding from a cut just under his eye.

Byrne smiled as he recognised the look of fear in the wounded man's face, and gently cradled the aching bulge in the crotch of his own trousers.

He paid no attention to the cars that sped by on the busy motorway. This was his turf.

The policeman's moment of self-absorbed sadism, however, was quickly interrupted.

'Byrne! There's a problem with the radio,' Wallis shouted over the rumble of motorway traffic.

'What kind of problem?' Byrne grunted, angry for the distraction.

'I can't get through. It's just static on all channels,' Wallis called back. 'My phone's the same. Try yours.'

Byrne grasped his radio in annoyance and made a call to the station. Just as Wallis had described, radio hiss faded in and out with a mixture of half spoken words. Feedback and broken sentences flooded together to produce an incomprehensible sea of babble that seemed to undulate like the flow of coastal tides.

'Good. We are close,' Taal broke his silence.

'So you can speak English!' Byrne snapped.

The furious policeman strode over to Taal, his feet pounding the ground with anger, his hands balled into fists, ready to vent his violent frustrations.

'You fucking little shit,' he screamed in the direction of the old man. 'You Paki fucker, I'm goi-'

His insults were cut short as he halted in his tracks, frozen like the universe in Taal's vision. The aged Servant of the Sacred Whisper had risen to his feet and calmly outstretched his left arm. Four of his fingers were held in differing angles and his lips moved slowly, recounting unheard words. Byrne's eyes widened to an unseen terror and his skin drained to a marble white. His legs began to shake, desperate to take him away from where he stood, but powerless to comply with this command. The policeman's stomach gurgled and his crotch grew damp, a darkening patch spread across his trousers revealing the urine that escaped his bladder. As piss ran down his leg he blinked and found the strength to break free from the trance.

Byrne ran to the police-marked BMW for protection, in the midst of a wild panic, and dropped to his knees. His stomach convulsed expelling its bile saturated contents. He tried to wipe the expelled stomach juices from his cheeks but vomited again. As it jettisoned from his mouth the repulsive cocktail of stomach acid and semi-digested food splashed onto his trousers; remnants hung off his lips in strands. He tried to spit them away, but to no avail.

'Are you okay?' Wallis knelt down beside him, torn between feelings of sympathy and disgust.

Byrne turned to face his colleague, tear stains marked his cheeks whilst snot dribbled from his nose. He spoke with a mouthful of saliva, his syllables lacking definition as he kept his jaw half open at all times, anxious to avoid the acrid taste of stomach lining.

'Put them in the car,' he motioned to Wallis with exaggerated movements, his speech rendered to the pronunciation of a small child. 'Put them in the car and take them into the city. Drop them by the fountains, they'll make their own way from there.'

'But they were headed to Newcastle,' Wallis questioned.

Byrne spat out another mouthful of vomit. 'The

truck was, they weren't.'

'Huh?' Wallis looked at his sickly partner in bewilderment. 'How did you know-'

'Just do as I say,' Byrne snapped before turning and vomiting again. 'Leave me here and get them into the city.' The pathetic mess of a police officer pointed a puke covered hand at Taal but turned his head, not daring to look directly at the small Indian figure, 'I'm not going anywhere near that freak again.'

SIX

Grinning as he spoke, Knight's voice snaked through the darkness leaving a wake of unease. 'Of course you want our help. Of course you want to know,' his velvet tones licked the air.

Kayleigh placed her back against the wall and slid into a sitting position, cowering as her trembling hands half covered her ears. His words gripped her stomach, making it churn with the echo of every syllable, but still she listened, torn between a hypnotic fascination and thought-numbing dread. She thought about leaving, imagining herself running back up the stairs, into the daylight and the protection of Ollie, but her curiosity rooted her to the spot.

How did he know me?

How did he know about my dream? I hadn't told anybody, but he knew details. Things only I…

Knight was still tied firmly to the chair with his left hand brutally hacked from his wrist. But despite being captive and wounded his presence held a threatening grip in the cold, disused basement. An air of menace radiated from the hunched figure, whilst his stocky frame appeared to swell in size like a creeping shadow, the edges of his faint silhouette flickered in the dark, like black fire against a starless night.

'Who are you?' Kayleigh cried out as her eyes widened, trying to make sense of the half sights she caught in the gloom.

Knight's smile grew as he tasted her fear.

'Who am I? What does it matter?' his mouth curled beneath the sunglasses that rested on the bridge of his nose. 'What am I?' he sneered.

His voice clawed at her thoughts as the sound bounced off the cracked plasterboard and exposed brickwork, echoing round the room in a disorientating fashion; his final sentence emanating from behind her.

Shocked by the unnatural approach of Knight's whisper, Kayleigh tried to scream but her breath was lost in fright, leaving nothing more than a muted gasp. Narrowing her eyes to force a better focus through her glasses, she made him out in the gloom. He was still in front of her, still captive in the chair. The sight both reassured and unnerved the confused seventeen year old.

'What are you…?' Kayleigh's voice struggled to rise from her throat and trailed off, unsure of her own words.

'The things we do, Kayleigh. The things we know,' Knight's speech came at the girl from every direction, drifting from the right, then left.

Above her, behind her, below her, his voice bled through the black, seemingly coming from everywhere at once; from the furthest corners of the room and, simultaneously, a gentle brush behind her ear.

'The things we have seen,' he continued. 'We can show you. I can show you. It's all behind my eyes.'

A trail of thick blood, black in the dim light, had pooled on the floor from Knight's wound and edged its path towards the girl. It lapped against her fingers as they rested on the ground. Kayleigh pulled her hand close as she felt the liquid on her skin. Immediately her digits began to sting with a deep, cold burn, rapidly spreading into the flesh and penetrating to the marrow of her bone. Shaking off the thick, black substance, she wrapped her hand in her sleeve and held it close to her chest, warming it against her own body heat.

She shook her head in disbelief. Fear was distorting her mind, warping her senses to the point of insanity. Sound was bending direction, shadows were growing in the dark, blood was burning cold.

What was happening?

'You're curious, aren't you?' Knight cooed with a soothing tone of temptation.

Kayleigh cautiously rose to her feet and looked around for the stairs. The darkness either side eclipsed her view, concealing what lay only a few feet away.

Which way had she come in?

She tried to cast her mind back to when she'd fumbled down the steps, when an unnameable calling, a curiosity that sung on the breeze, pulled her from her fear and back to the darkened belly of the building.

That had been only been a few minutes ago.

Why couldn't she remember?!

'I know you, Kayleigh.'

Knight's voice saturated the young girl's mind,

flooding her frustrated thoughts. She looked one way, then the other, but could see nothing through the darkness.

Which way was the stairs?!

Unable to pin-point the exit, Kayleigh took a chance, turned to her right and ran, desperate to leave the basement and flee Knight's presence; desperate to get him out of her head.

But escape was not so easily found as she slammed into a solid brick wall.

Recovering from the collision, Kayleigh groped wildly for a doorway, finding nothing but impassable masonry.

'I know you want to know,' Knight's voice trickled into her ears, past the thumping sound of her own heartbeat as it echoed through her skull. 'I can feel your desire.'

She turned and ran in the opposite direction, colliding into the cold, hard stone of another wall. Her chin caught a jagged edge of plasterboard that still clung to the remains of the building's inner shell. It grazed her skin, causing blood to seep, slowly from the wound.

'You want to know about your dream.'

Kayleigh ran her hands along the scuffed and damaged wall, but found no exit. The staircase simply wasn't there. Confused and disorientated she banged her fists against the fired clay.

'What's going on? Ollie!' Kayleigh called out, hoping her friend would hear her. 'Ollie!' she screamed as she fell to the floor.

Unable to leave, she tried to block out her hostage's words but she found it impossible, and as if she were futilely trying to fight the tide, she finally gave in, letting his words wash through her.

'I can help you, Kayleigh,' Knight's poisonously mellifluous rasp continued. 'I know about your dream last night. I know how you dream of unicorns. How you dance with them in the forests of your thoughts. But last night was different. Last night the unicorn didn't dance with you.'

Kayleigh closed her eyes tightly and covered her ears, trying to block out his words once more. As she squeezed her eyelids closed, patterns swirled in her enforced darkness.

Flashes of eyes.

Red and hateful.

Then black.

Cold and evil.

The muffled sound of hooves galloped in the air between her ears and palms. Her hands clamped harder against her head in an effort to silence it.

The harder she tried to block it out, the louder the sound grew.

'When exactly did you wake up, Kayleigh?' Knight's words found their way through too.

She felt warm breath on the back of her neck.

Her stomach hurt.

'Did you wake up before the long horn between its angry, evil eyes pierced your flesh? Or did you stay asleep that little longer? Did you feel the horn drive through your stomach? Did you feel it raise its head and puncture your lung? Did you feel your breath go shallow and the blood drain from your body? Did you feel it pierce your heart?'

Kayleigh clutched at her stomach.

'Did you feel yourself die?'

A tear gently crept from her eye and rolled down the pale skin of her cheek as she remembered scrabbling through the grass, clawing back the undergrowth as she tried frantically to out run the chasing beast.

Kayleigh opened her eyes and uncovered her ears.

A haunting stillness filled her mind. Like watching an explosion in slow motion, she felt at once terrified and at the same time captivated by the memory of the vision she had first encountered in her sleep. Although stood at its centre she was like an impassioned by-stander, unable to exert any influence, but painfully aware of what was to come.

'Do you know why that happened?' Knight spoke as he watched her get to her feet. 'I can show you. It's all in my eyes. Take a look. Lift up my glasses and see. Look into my eyes.'

'I could have sworn I saw them.'

Ollie was pacing back and forth, trying to recall the blurred events that had got them here.

The chase from the cops.

Stumbling into the guys in suits.

Guys and girls.

He swore there had been two women but looking across the construction site he could only see one at the meeting point. *Where was the other one?*

Had there even been another one?

The adrenalin had reduced his memories to a series of half remembered flashes. Snatches of faces and fists. Screeches of tyres and deafening gunshots. It had been a matter of minutes, maybe even less before they'd bundled into Sam's passing van. No time to capture detail.

Why the hell were they packing guns anyway? And what was in that case?

They'd tried so hard to open it. Bricks, metal piping, even a hacksaw from Sam's van had all been used as tools in attempts to open the briefcase, but the locks refused to give. They were strange locks too, a series of holes and symbols dotted the metal fastenings making them seem more decorative than functional.

Whatever was in that case the owners wanted it back, badly.

It was all such a mess.

If the man with the briefcase handcuffed to his wrist hadn't accidentally been pushed into the van and knocked unconscious as they clambered for their escape, they wouldn't even be in this situation.

If Sam's tool bag had been packed with anything more than a hacksaw and some loose screws maybe they could have armed themselves.

If Laura hadn't been taken, if Sam hadn't acted so wild, they could have all just walked away.

Ollie berated himself for going over the *what-ifs;* they weren't going to help him and his friends now.

He thought back to the man tied up in the basement and shook his head as he recounted the psychotic mania that had filled Sam. Did it really happen? Was his friend really capable and willing to cut someone's hand off? He still couldn't believe it.

And throughout the whole thing the guy didn't stir; not once. That kind of pain should have woken him up;

driving him from his unconscious state with an ear splitting scream. But if he did come round he didn't show it. He didn't make a sound; didn't move a muscle.

The whole, blood soaked episode just didn't feel real. Like the chase and gunshots before, the detail had rapidly dissolved making it feel more like a dream.

Sanity had long since left them. Reality seemed to be doing the same.

A shriek echoed through the disused building, pulling Ollie from his fragmented reflections. The scream made him jump with fright, its tone of pure terror resonating with the inner fear he'd been trying hard to suppress.

'Kayleigh!' he cried and ran into the darkness of the building.

Turning left, down the corridor, he headed towards the stairs of the basement but was knocked to the floor by a powerful blow. Ollie landed hard on his back, the wind forced from his lungs. As he climbed to his feet he felt the panicked hands of Kayleigh, trembling and gripping his arms tightly. Her pale white face, stripped of colour by fear, faintly glowed in the surrounding gloom.

'Kayleigh, are you okay?' Ollie put his arms around her but she wriggled free of the attempted hug. 'I didn't mean to run into you.'

'His… his… his… his eyes,' she spluttered in barely coherent syllables.

Ollie gripped both her arms in an attempt to stop her shaking. The terrified teenager looked directly into her friend's face with a stare that looked straight through him.

'What's up?' Ollie asked.

'I can't stay here. I've got to go,' Kayleigh pushed past him.

Ollie caught her hand, trying to stop the terrified girl, but she pulled herself free from his loose grip and ran down the corridor, out of the abandoned building and into the light.

He scratched his head in confusion, unsure of what had gotten into her. Maybe it had all been too much. She was only young.

Leaving his friend to find her own comfort he turned back towards the point where the corridor fell to its most inky black. This was the entrance to the darkened stairwell; the descending passageway that led to the basement. Something inside him responded to an invisible call, a yearning to understand what Kayleigh had saw. It was a ridiculous notion, and yet it was impossible to fight. He took his phone out of his pocket, using the screen as a makeshift torch. It did little to light the way, but did enough to show him the edge of each step as he made his way down to the depths of the building, following a curiosity that gripped at his heart.

SEVEN

Rasping interference wrestled with the sound of a panicked and fraught female voice.

'Plea- -elp uh-,' crackled from the speaker of a stolen police radio amidst the whir and whine of static. Her words were lost in the swamp of sound, resulting in barely intelligible syllables.

Scullin squeezed the radio tightly and looked towards Jake, watching the horror grow on his face as he slowly recognised the terrified voice that fought through the white noise.

'Her partner was left to die. To bleed out in the back of a car,' Scullin said throwing the radio to the ground. 'But your sister will do it in front of an audience.'

Regretting he'd ever listened to Scullin and let the woman live, it didn't take Duell long to stride with purposeful steps up the dusty slope of the building site and back to the limousine. It had been parked in haste, by the side of a condemned and crumbling two storey building; concealed enough to keep it hidden, but allowing for an advantageous view over the agreed meeting point. He kept his vision focused on the metallic black, luxury vehicle as he made his approach.

If it had been his decision the policewoman would have been killed outright a long time ago and left on the side of the street. At least now, finally, his murderous desires would be indulged.

Everything looked just the way he'd left it. Both cars had their doors shut, and trying one of the handles of the limo, he found it was still locked. He smiled as he glanced towards the Audi before pressing his forehead against the glass of the limousine. Duell peered through the window but was unable to see past the tinting.

Taking the key from his pocket he pressed a button. A whirring from the car indicated the doors were unlocking. Cautiously he gripped a door handle and, pulling it up with controlled patience, he waited a moment.

Waiting for a reaction.

When nothing happened he slowly opened the door.

Blood trickled from the car and onto the ground, splashing the polished leather of his shoes. Duell looked at the dead policeman slumped over the back seat. A cracked and broken radio lay on the lap of the corpse, rasping an undulating hiss through its speaker. Ducking down, Duell edged his head into the limousine to get a better view of the scene.

With no time to defend himself, the heavy boot of Special Constable Forrest caught his cheek, knocking him to the ground. Rising to his feet, he didn't have a chance to look up and watch his assailant step from the car before another boot struck him directly between the legs. Duell landed on his knees as his mouth screwed into a grimace. Forrest kicked again, but this time he was ready for her. Thrusting his hand out, he caught her ankle, twisting it over and deflecting the blow. Fluidly, he followed the motion and threw her to the ground.

Aimee rolled over to face him and punched out as she did so, hitting his stomach and knocking the wind from his lungs. She scrabbled to her feet but was caught before she could stand by the surprising speed and agility of her adversary. His long, spindly fingers clamped either side of her head and pulled her face, at rapid knots, towards his knee.

Aimee instinctively turned in his grip, rolling to the side to protect herself. Duell's bony kneecap glanced the back of her neck as the Special Constable crashed to the floor.

Viciously he kicked at the side of the prone woman, connecting hard with her ribs. Grabbing her neck, and with unnatural strength, he lifted her clean off the ground and began to throttle her. Gasping for breath, Aimee tried to kick out but was thrown through the air, colliding with one of the reinforced windows of the Audi. Dazed and reeling from the blow she tried to find her feet but her balance had deserted her; the world spinning in wild rotations before her eyes.

Pathetically she stumbled on her knees as she heard the mocking leer of Duell above her.

'I lost my gun in the brawl earlier today. But I didn't need it to beat you. You're lucky we let you live as long as we did,' the sound of his voice felt like the cold claw of anaesthetic. 'Scullin wants me to take you back to the others. To torture you in front of your own brother. But you've given me the perfect excuse to end this here. I would have killed you a long time ago, so let's enjoy this. Let's make this slow.'

Aimee tried again to stand, but her legs would not obey. She fell onto the dusty, clay ground, landing hard on all fours.

Trying to focus on one spot, she watched Duell's blood-splattered shoes come into her blurred and unsettled vision. He cast a shadow over her, sending a shiver through her body. She was defenceless, unable to look up, let alone protect herself against the next attack.

'You have quite the fighting spirit in you,' he drawled in a tone that although sounded emotionless and detached, was unable to hide a ravenous anticipation. 'I'm going to savour your essence.'

Through the carousel of her spinning vision Aimee saw Duell's sunglasses drop to the floor, landing by his feet. She tried to look up, but couldn't move, the dizziness too debilitating for her to do anything but wait for his next assault.

She closed her eyes tightly as he unleashed a guttural scream, forcing her to clench her teeth. Aimee thought about her family, about her parents, about her brother. She hoped they'd be safe.

Everything fell silent.

She braced herself as she waited for the final blow.

'Leave my sister alone,' Jake shouted, enraged.

'I'm afraid it's far too late for that,' Scullin replied,

his words causing vomit to climb Jake's quivering throat. 'She's in one of our cars, and not looking too well if I recall. Don't worry, you'll get to say goodbye. That is, unless Duell gets carried away. He can be so over eager.'

Scullin shot a glance to a grinning Cross who beamed with a knowing smile as she wiped Laura's blood across her lips. She choked the nineteen year old as a warning to the others, squeezing Laura's neck and forcing the scratch marks to pour with more crimson liquid.

'He's not the only one,' Cross laughed.

After a moment Aimee opened her eyes, and as the dizziness began to lift, her focus found its clarity. Aimee eyed the feet in front of her, noticing that the blood splashed shoes had been replaced with a pair of boots. A pair of Magnum Hi –Top's, just like hers.

Turning her head to the side she looked across to see Duell, motionless and sprawled out, face down in the dirt; his arms and legs spread at unnatural angles. She squinted through the clearing haze of her correcting sight to see something on top of Duell's head.

No, not on top, *through* Duell's head.

A steel support rod, twisted and still with one end firmly attached to a block of concrete, had been driven straight through her attacker's cranium. The rod glistened with a hint of crimson, coated in fleshy fragments of brain matter. His blonde hair dyed red.

The wires of a taser protruded from his body, leading to a gun that lay in the dust.

Aimee looked back at the boots in front of her. Slowly she raised her head, following the line of the crease that had been carefully ironed into the dark blue trousers. The uniform was a familiar one that ended with a friendly face and reassuring smile. The man crouched down beside her.

'It's Forrest, isn't it?' the police officer asked, offering a hand to help her up.

'Aimee, that's right,' she replied as she gripped his palm and pulled herself to her feet, resting against the limousine for support.

'I'm PC Pritchard,' his smile widening, revealing a perfect set of gleaming white teeth. 'You can call me Paul.'

Paul took her shoulders and steadied her, then turned back and studied the dead body on the ground.

'Shit, I didn't mean to kill him,' he scratched his head as he thought back through the last few moments. 'I fired the taser to stop him, but he fell onto that post. Ah fuck.'

'He's dead alright,' Aimee responded. 'But it was either me or him. Thank you.'

Paul bent down and rummaged through Duell's pockets.

'Nothing,' he sounded dejected. 'No wallet, no ID, no gun. Who is he?'

'Not a clue,' Aimee responded. 'And he's not alone. What's that?' she pointed to the other car. 'I could have sworn I saw something in there.'

PC Pritchard tried the door to the Audi.

'Locked,' he confirmed as it refused to open. 'Hello, is there anyone there?' he called through the tinted glass. *Must have been a reflection*, he thought before turning his attention to the other vehicle and ducking his head into the back of the limousine.

'What happened in here?' he exclaimed. 'Oh shit. Oh God.' His voice soften with sadness, 'Isn't this PC Osborne?'

'Yes, it is,' Aimee looked down at her feet, unable to rest her eyes back on the body of her friend.

'I'm pretty new to this city, didn't know him that well,' Paul explained. 'But from what I've heard he was a really good guy.'

'He was one of the best,' she felt unfallen tears glaze her eyes with grief, but fought them back.

'I'm sorry,' her saviour said as he rubbed her shoulder in sympathy. 'What's going on here?'

Special Constable Forrest did her best to describe the events of the morning. She explained how she and PC Osborne had been on patrol when they chased a gang that had been shoplifting. They hadn't been in pursuit long when the gang had ran into a group of men and women escorting a man carrying a briefcase. The two groups fought and in the scuffle shots were fired. They escaped with their lives, but hostages were taken on both sides. Whilst the fleeing gang had ended up with the briefcase and its carrier, one of the girls was left behind with the gun carrying civilians. The two constables had been caught in the gunfire, PC Osborne was hit badly several times, whilst Forrest had been lucky. A graze across the temple had knocked her unconscious but nothing more serious than that.

'I can only guess we were taken hostage too, they gave chase and we ended up here,' PC Forrest concluded.

'Then you're lucky to be alive,' PC Pritchard

remarked. 'Twice.'

'I guess God is looking favourably on me today,' she smiled as she thought back to Osborne. His words through her. Repeating them made her feel closer to him, like part of him was being kept alive.

'You're lucky I heard your message. The radios have been all messed up today,' Paul's friendly smile returned. 'I was heading back to the station to see what was what, when I caught fragments of your distress call. I couldn't make out much, but thankfully the part I caught was your location.'

'I'm so glad you did,' Aimee flashed a grin of thanks. 'We've got to help these dumb kids out. Do you think anyone else is coming?'

The smile faded from Paul's face, 'I doubt it. With all this weird interference we'd be lucky if anyone else heard you. It looks we're on our own.'

EIGHT

Another growl of thunder clawed at the unsettled sky, its low frequencies reverberating through the walls of the abandoned buildings. Knight heard the faint sound in the dank basement where he was held captive. He looked towards the ceiling and his grin grew wider. Rising to his feet he puffed out his chest and pulled his arms apart, freeing himself as the ropes that bound him snapped like cotton. The room grew darker as even the tiniest traces of light seemed to sliver out of existence, retreating in his presence.

'Your man's been a while,' Sam barked.

Scullin ground his teeth in annoyance, crushing the discarded police radio under foot.

'Sam, stop making him angry,' Eleanor spoke softly but with a tone of annoyance, one she'd heard her father use many times with her.

Laughing off her comments, Sam barked again, 'Maybe your man's bitten of more than he can chew.

Maybe the cops are already here waiting for the right time to charge down and fuck you up!'

'Enough,' Scullin seethed as he walked forward.

With a powerful strike of his hand he knocked Eleanor to the ground and took Sam by the throat, silencing his tirade. Cross laughed as Sam struggled in the choke hold and Eleanor held her throbbing cheek.

'Jake,' Laura called out with an expression of pure hatred for her boyfriend, 'help your friends. Do something!'

'Radio communication will come back up,' Special Constable Forrest sounded hopeful. 'It's probably some sort of technical glitch. They'll have it fixed soon, I'm sure.'

'Well I hope so,' PC Pritchard replied, his tone less sure than his colleagues. 'If those goons have guns we'll need back up. I don't fancy rushing down there without armed response.'

'We can't just leave those kids there,' Aimee protested.

Aimee couldn't help but refer to them as kids, despite them all growing up. Jake and his friends had been a part of their family life for as long as she could remember. Even when they'd finished school they didn't drift off and move away as others had done. The gang stuck together, unemployed or working crummy jobs, they still lived in the same council block. They were jokingly called *The Stills*. *Still* living at home, *still* not got a job, *still* hanging round with your deadbeat mates.

They were directionless and their boredom took them into pursuits at odds with Aimee's policing. But she hoped her new vocation would rub off on her brother and his friends; provide them with a sliver of inspiration. To her they were all family and she cared for them deeply.

'We won't leave them,' Paul assured her. 'My car is just a little way up here. We'll get up on higher ground and see if we can call through to control. Like you said, I'm sure they'll have the radios fixed soon.'

Aimee knew Paul was talking sense, but as she walked up to the perimeter of the construction site she looked back toward the stand-off with a feeling of guilt. She should be walking towards them, not away.

She'd already witnessed two people die today, there would not be any more.

Ollie shuffled down the stairs, unsteady in the darkness. The screen from his phone did a poor job at offering illumination, decreasing in power the further he went, forcing him to feel for the edge of each step in turn. His journey had been slow and steady, taking so long he wondered if he'd gotten lost along the way. But as he felt through the gloom he reasoned there was only one route and the dark can play tricks on the mind. A curious pull continued to drag him forward, undiminished by the fear that edged his thoughts.

The air in the basement felt unclean; stale and old. Ollie took a deep breath and stifled the resulting cough as the musty atmosphere tickled his throat.

He shone the dim, blue glow of his make-shift torch around the room, exposing the monochromatic outline of a chair, knocked to the floor and leaning on its own back rest; the metal poles of its legs angled toward the ceiling.

Ollie's heart pounded against his rib cage.

Where was the hostage?

Sweeping his light across the floor he saw trails of black glisten against the glow of the phone. Lengths of discarded rope littered the floor like resting vipers.

A flash of movement caught Ollie's eye. He shone his torch in the perceived direction but the light did little to penetrate the engulfing blackness. Shapes appeared to writhe out of the darkness, black on black, offering no definite sense of form but suggesting… something. He felt a presence but wherever he turned he saw nothing; nothing but the same crowded emptiness. It was as if the darkness itself was alive, teeming with formless terrors that screamed silently, unravelling the bravery and curiosity with which Ollie had made his descent into the basement.

Walking backwards he stumbled over the upturned chair, catching his balance before he fell. He'd only saw Kayleigh leave which meant the guy with the severed hand was still down here. Somewhere.

He held his breath, straining to listen for a sound that might give away the man's location.

A faint creaking floated through the room, a slow deliberate scratching, the gentle laughter of a child.

What?!

Ollie's skin prickled with fear and his mind raced with unfathomable answers as he catalogued the barely audible sounds that punctuated the stillness; their sources incoherent in a room so dark, direction had lost all relevance.

A gentle gust of wind, the ticking of a clock, the

mewling of a new born lamb.

He slowly stepped through the basement, trying to remember where he'd entered, trying to find the staircase that would lead him out of this surreal scene. As an uneasy dread clambered through his thoughts his calm disintegrated; not due to one definable incident, but down to the multitude of creeps that swamped his brain. Unnameable nightmares filled his head, faceless feelings of terror plucked at his nerves, growing and consuming his thoughts until he could stand it no more.

The sounds, as subtle as their volume was, overwhelmed him.

The hiss of a snake, the crackle of fire, the terminal cough of his Grandmother.

Grandma Elsie had been a habitual smoker and died of lung cancer when Ollie was only nine years old. The sound of her terrible, hacking cough had disturbed him greatly as a child. He'd always thought he could hear her dying, piece by piece as she seemed to rot away from the inside. Each splutter had made him clench his teeth with hatred for the disease that ravaged her. Each cough would bring silent tears rolling down his face. He'd never forgotten that sound, and although he'd never hear it again after her death, his nightmares kept it alive, giving it a deeper, threatening resonance.

How was he hearing it here, in a disused basement?

His body turned cold and a tear fell down his cheek. His jaw clenched and Ollie ran. He didn't know if he was going the right way, and didn't care. He just needed to escape. He would have dug through the walls with his bare hands if he needed too.

Hurtling through the blackness his journey seemed

to last forever as he careered head long into the dark. His legs shook from under him as they burned with exhaustion, crumpling beneath his weight when he was knocked to the floor by a powerful and unseen blow.

His phone flew from his hand and skidded across the floor, the light from the screen fading as it smashed against a wall.

Special Constable Aimee Forrest sat in the passenger seat of PC Pritchard's police car, leaving the door open and allowing the breeze to circulate in an attempt to remain cool. The air was hot and sticky, and the gathering wind was just as humid, providing little respite.

'Is he okay?' she asked, nodding her head back towards the figure that sat, cuffed in the back of the car.

'That is Sergeant Bryne,' PC Pritchard replied. 'He's a traffic cop I picked up this morning. His colleague waved me down, said the guy was going nuts.'

'He looks in a bad way,' Aimee eyed his puke splattered uniform. Bile had dried onto the fabric leaving yellow crusts that trailed down his front.

Byrne had his eyes to the ceiling and rocked gently, muttering inaudible words over and over.

'He's been harmless since we got him into the car. Poor sod,' Paul scratched his head. 'God knows what he's taken, or maybe something just snapped inside.'

'Even in this state he looks pretty mean,' Aimee replied. 'I'm glad of the partition.'

She tapped the metal grill that separated the front seats from the back. Byrne glanced at her with unfocused eyes before returning to his fixed gaze at a point somewhere above him.

Unaware of the detainee's disturbance Aimee looked across the bowl-like dimensions of the Oracle shopping centre building site; her vision focused through a gap in the crumbling buildings and barely standing walls, making out the people stood in its centre. From this distance they were barely anything more than silhouettes, unidentifiable figures only inches high.

What were they doing down there?

She grew impatient. This was wasting time.

Ollie got back to his feet as his eyes tried their best to adjust to the blanket of darkness. The adrenalin surged through his body, increasing the power of his senses to a point of near disorientation. The sounds grew louder and the musty, damp smell was so strong he could taste it on his tongue. His vision though, improved as it was, still remained limited.

In the darkness, about eight feet away, he made out a faint shimmer of white. The more he focused on it the more sense it began to make. The glow came from a shirt, the part exposed from the opening of a suit jacket.

It was the white shirt worn by their hostage.

It was Knight.

Without any time to react, Knight came charging towards him, swinging a fist and knocking him across the room. Ollie landed hard on the cracked, tiled floor, his side catching the end from one of the chair legs that stuck up like a set of spikes. He held his stinging wound and felt his t-shirt grow damp with blood.

'Oooo, that smells good,' Knight taunted in the blackness. 'If my tastes were more base I'd be salivating.'

Ollie got to his feet but kept low, trying his best to

stay hidden in the dark.

'You can't hide from me, Ollie,' Knight continued, 'this is my domain. You and your friends stumbled into something that did not concern you. But now it does. Maybe it always did.'

Ollie felt along the floor, his hands searching for a weapon, anything with which he could use to defend himself.

'You talk a lot,' his courage was renewed when his fingers found Sam's broken, blooded saw blade. 'I never believed in fate.'

'Fate is a simple concept, Ollie,' Knight stalked through the darkness.

Ollie tried to keep a watchful eye on the shimmer of his shirt but it was swallowed up in the mirk; fading out of view, only to reappear again somewhere completely different, moments later.

'I'm talking of something far more intricate. Something less tangible, but much more real,' Knight continued.

Even following his voice was no help, its source and direction seemed to be entirely independent to the location of the glow from his clothing. Ollie held the blade in front of him, ready to attack.

'Where's the girl?' Knight asked. 'Where's Kayleigh?'

PC Pritchard gave up on his attempts to fight over the squall of the radio's hiss. He turned to his colleague and tried his best to hide his frustrations.

'Still no good,' he said, clipping the radio back onto his vest.

Aimee did not turn to face him, her focus remained on the group in the distance.

'We need to get down there,' she spoke with impatience. 'I can't wait any longer. Something's going on. They've already gotten themselves into enough trouble.'

'We could drive back to the station,' Paul offered. 'Get some back up that way.'

'We've already wasted enough time,' she spoke with considered authority. Her doubts of being a good cop had been washed away by the adrenalin coursing through her body. This was not the time for doubts and inaction. 'We have to get them out of there, now.'

'Come on, Forrest, that's crazy talk. We'd just provoke the situation,' PC Pritchard tried to reason with her.

'You don't understand, Paul,' she turned to face him. 'I don't have any choice, that's my-'

A banging on the car bonnet cut her sentence short as they both turned to see the source of the commotion.

A girl with long, auburn hair looked at the pair through the windscreen. Her face was pale white behind her glasses, her purple painted fingernails pressed into the bodywork of the car as her hands trembled, matching the shaking that possessed her entire being.

'Kayleigh!'

'She's a very special girl you know?'

'You leave her alone,' Ollie shouted.

'That's not possible. Not anymore,' Knight's voice appeared behind him.

Ollie swung out with the saw blade, but found no

target. The bloodied blade sliced through the empty air.

'Stop hiding, you bastard,' Ollie's rage grew at the frustration of not getting a clean shot.

'What makes you think I'm hiding?' Knight stated matter-of-factly. 'I'm right here.'

Ollie turned to see Knight stood inches from him. The large, suited man swung a fist sending the boy flying, but not before he launched the toothed blade at his attacker. The sharp teeth of the workman's tool cut through the cloth of his jacket and dug, deep into his flesh. For a moment Knight seemed clearer in the dark, more visible, as he gripped the blade and pulled it from his arm. The sound of blood splashing on the floor echoed round the basement but Knight made no reaction to the injury.

'You want some more of that shit?' Ollie taunted, knowing full well he had no weapon to back up his idle threat. 'If you don't want any more of that you'd best let me walk out of here.'

'You couldn't find your way out if I let you,' Knight mocked.

'Yeah? I'm willing to give that a go,' Ollie put his back against the wall and edged round the room. If he could keep the guy talking he might be able to distract him long enough to find the stairs. 'So what are you guys? Some kind of black ops Government agency? You got that whole *Men In Black/Agent Smith* look down.'

'Your Governments mean little to us,' came the response. 'Only their power.'

'Not Government. Then some kind of Illuminati thing. New World Order type shit?' Ollie made his way to the corner of the room. His fingers felt over crumbling plasterboard and thick, dust ridden cobwebs as he continued along the next wall in search of the exit.

'A new world? You have no idea,' Knight sounded annoyed by this line of questioning. 'Who we are is of little importance to you. As you are of little importance to me.'

'Now, come on, I'm not *that* unimportant,' Ollie did his best to keep the distraction going. The more time he could stall for, the more time he had to find his escape. 'I'm a pretty mean drummer. You want to rock out? I could help you rock out. You wait until you hear my band. You'll be loosening your tie and getting your ass down in the mosh pit. A man with your pain tolerance would do well in a *wall of death*.'

'Enough of this. My amusement fades,' Knight shouted in anger from the darkness. 'The only death you need to be concerned with is your own!'

He didn't stand a chance as Knight appeared, without warning, from the gloom and gripped Ollie by the throat. As he began crushing his windpipe, Knight lifted Ollie off the ground, his feet dangling helplessly in the air.

Gasping for breath, Ollie swung his legs, kicking at Knight's ribs. His assailants frame felt as hard as stone and appeared unaffected by the counter attack. He gripped at Knight's fingers and tried to prise them from his neck, but his digits felt strange; long and muscular with a slimy, yet bony hold. Ollie raked at the abnormal, skinless texture, realising Knight had him held by his left hand.

But that can't be, he thought. *That was the hand Sam had…*

Ollie lashed out, his brain driven crazy as thoughts of the impossible swirled around his head. He clawed at Knight's face and in doing so knocked his sunglasses to the floor. The darkness obscured the detail but despite this he could still tell something wasn't right. There was something unnatural about the contours of Knight's face, something he hadn't noticed before. The way light and dark bounced off his profile, distorted and warped. The twisted shadows that collected round his eyes.

Knight pulled Ollie closer.

Oh my God, his eyes, Ollie thought as his view became clearer.

Things began to twist and bend in the gloom.

An eerie moan, like gales of wind, grew to deafening decibels.

Ollie roared with defiant courage as his body shook in violent spasms. Still held aloft by Knight, his body grew damp as blood seeped from the pores of his skin.

He tried one last time to escape the deathly clutches of the choke hold, but he was too weak. Thick, crimson liquid ran from his body, pouring from his eyes and ears. He tried to swallow only to gag on the metallic taste as it filled his throat. His eyeballs lost shape as they slowly began to liquefy, melting into a putrid mess that oozed down his cheeks. His tongue began to blister, swelling with sores that filled his mouth. The blisters expanded like vile bubbles until they burst, erupting their pus-filled contents. The taste coated his mouth and his stomach tightened. He choked on the thick, foul liquid, as it ran down his throat. He spluttered and coughed but the gag reflex did nothing to abate the torrent of fluid as it filled his lungs, drowning him in a vile cocktail of pustule discharge and silencing him forever.

Aimee leapt from the car and took hold of the young girl, pulling her into an embrace of reassurance.

Kayleigh collapsed into the Special Constable's arms. For a moment Aimee held her, tenderly caressing her back in comfort before she pulled her out of the hug, bringing their eyes level.

'Kayleigh, what happened?' she asked.

'I - I - I… He knew. He knew everything,' Kayleigh's words fell from a confused mind, her words fought through panicked breaths.

'Who? What do you mean?' Aimee tried to get some sense from her ramblings.

'The one we got. The one Ollie's keeping a watch on. In there,' the distressed girl pointed to one of the crumbling buildings, across the craters and urban wasteland to the other side of the perimeter.

'What did he know?' Aimee enquired.

Kayleigh looked deep into the Special Constable's eyes and momentarily calmed. 'My dream,' she said, sounding surprised by her own words.

'Where's Jake?' Aimee asked.

'He's there,' Kayleigh pointed to the distant figures in the centre, her voice quivering with a fresh onslaught of emotion. 'He's trying to sort this. But he can't. You've got to help them!' she said erupting into tears and crying into her comforter's shoulder.

'Wait, you know this girl?' Paul asked, approaching the pair.

'Yes, I know her. I know most of them,' Forrest turned to Paul. 'As much as it pains me, one of those *kids* is Jake Forrest, my younger brother. I have to help them.'

'But we need back up,' Paul repeated. 'They're armed and dangerous.'

'Look, very soon they are going to question where their man has got to, the one you killed, and that's going to make them itchy. You stay up here with Kayleigh and keep trying to get through, get that back up arranged,' she commanded. 'I'll head down there, get closer and keep a watch over things. If it starts to escalate I'll come back to you and devise a plan. For the time being I'll keep out of sight, I promise. I can't just stand by while my little brother is in danger.'

'Forrest…' PC Pritchard felt the emotion in her voice, he knew it was useless to persuade her otherwise.

He took Kayleigh by the hand and offered gentle words of reassurance in an attempt to calm her down. Aimee surveyed the landscape, working out the best route to get close but not be seen. She was outnumbered and unarmed. Stealth was her only ally.

'Forrest,' PC Pritchard called out.

She turned to face him.

'Aimee, take this,' he threw a canister over the car, towards her.

Aimee caught the cylinder of PAVA. She remembered back to her training and the agony of being sprayed in the eyes with the incapacitating liquid. She'd never felt as much pain in her life as she did that day. Her eyes watered and itched at the excruciating memory.

'Thanks Paul,' she smiled, clutching the newly acquired weapon tightly in her hand.

Turning back to the group in the middle she set off

to get closer, carefully keeping herself to the edges of the crumbling buildings.

'If we get out of this, Jake,' she muttered to herself, 'I'm going to fucking kill you.'

Sam crumpled to the floor and screamed in agony holding his left hand by the wrist. His fingers bent at crooked angles and wept blood through jagged gashes, cut through the skin by the sharp edges of broken bones. Eleanor ran to where he lay, kneeling beside him and placing her arm around him for comfort. His face was ashen white and his body shook in her embrace.

'Holy shit,' she muttered, trying to keep her disgust from Sam. She looked towards Scullin and scowled.

'At least it's still attached,' Scullin scoffed before turning to Jake. 'Tell me where you've hidden Knight!' he boomed. 'Tell me where Knight and the key are!'

'I… I…' Jake stuttered.

'Jake,' Laura interrupted, her face softened as she pleaded with her lover. 'Tell him. It's okay. We can't let this go on. You can put a stop to it all right now.' Her voice cracked with the emotional weight her words possessed. 'I love you, Jake Forrest.'

He glanced over at Eleanor who nodded with approval, agreeing with her best friend.

'Over there,' Jake pointed to the building they'd done their best to hide. Earlier they'd taken a snaking path to the meeting place in an attempt to conceal their tracks. How futile that seemed now. 'In that building over there. He's in the basement.'

Laura smiled, but her display of affection did nothing to stop Jake breaking down, crying into his hands as he allowed the guilt of betraying his friends to overwhelm him.

Scullin, Cross and King nodded to each other and reached into their jackets.

NINE

Police sirens wailed through the air, but drifted away as quickly as they came, dashing Special Constable Forrest's hopes of assistance from her full time colleagues. Judging from the number of *blues and twos* that carried on the breeze as the squad cars screeched through the city this wasn't the only pocket of town that was going to hell.

Keeping herself low to avoid detection, she made her way across the construction site that was fast resembling a war zone with its littering of damaged vehicles and dead bodies. Reaching the building that Kayleigh had pointed out, she ducked inside. There were no working lights and her eyes took a moment to adjust to the dark. She felt a chill as the Special Constable walked further into the depths of the disused shell of a building.

'Ollie,' she whispered. 'Ollie, are you there? It's Aimee, Jake's sister. I'm here to help.' She paused and listened but heard no response. 'Kayleigh sent me,' she called, stopping to listen again.

Cautiously Aimee, headed down the stairs to the basement. As she reached the bottom her footsteps made the sound of gentle splashing, like she was walking though puddles. Crouching down, she dipped her fingers in to the liquid and brought the tips to her nostrils. Peering through the darkness she caught sight of several large objects littering the floor. An unsettling feeling gripped her stomach as her mind dwelt on what those objects might be. Moving closer to one of them she made out the shape of five digits; a set of fingers connected to a hand and arm. She traced the severed arm to its toned bicep and made out the familiar tattoo that snaked down it. The abstract image of Marilyn Monroe smiled in the darkness. The image's hat normally came across Ollie's shoulder and onto his chest, but a savage tear of flesh had cut the hat in two. Its frayed edges wept with the same liquid that covered the floor.

'Oh God, Ollie,' Aimee quietly gasped in horror.

The room was filled with his blood and the ground littered with limbs, *his limbs*; parts of his body brutally pulled to pieces and torn from each other by…

By what?

Could a man do this?

A blow to the side of her head sent the young Special Constable reeling. She looked back to the source of the attack and briefly saw a man, dressed in a suit with dark hair and dark sunglasses. He walked backwards into the shadow, his features enveloped by the black of the room.

Aimee squinted, searching for her mysterious

attacker.

Another blow landed square in her back, knocking her to the wall. Before she could defend herself she was punched again, just below her ribs. Aimee yelled in pain. Wet, slender fingers took hold of the back of her neck sending a curious sensation through her body; a wave of chills that proceeded a creeping numbness. The feeling oozed like treacle through her muscles, making her gasp as a sensation of drowning took hold of her senses.

Forrest thrust her elbow backwards into his arm, dislodging Knight's grip and freeing herself from the debilitating unease. Spinning round, she kicked out, hitting his knee, and although abnormally solid, his leg folded as her heavy boot caught it. Knight fell forward, receiving another boot to his stomach.

'You sick fuck,' Aimee scolded as she watched him drop to the floor.

She kicked out again, but this time Knight caught her foot as he unleashed an earnest scream that twisted her stomach in fear. Losing balance from the ear splitting shriek, Aimee was thrown forwards, landing in a crumpled heap.

The sound of running footsteps echoed through the basement as Knight sprinted towards the downed Constable. Catching sight of his raised fist, Aimee rolled, narrowly avoiding his knuckles as they crashed down. Just dodging the blow, she felt the ground beneath her crack as his iron-like fist hit the concrete floor.

How strong is this guy? she thought. *What kind of drugs is he taking?*

Forrest scrambled to her feet and hid behind a pillar, keeping her body as tight to the wall as she could.

The room descended into silence. A stillness, pregnant with danger, filled the air.

'You can't hide in the dark,' Knight warned. 'I am the dark.'

His voice drifted from a place unknown, then drifted off again, swallowed up by the oppressive hush.

In the distance, Aimee heard the sound of a baby crying. As the wailing grew louder it was joined by another, then another. More and more screaming babies called out in the darkness, a chorus of bawling infants floated on the air like a nightmarish melody.

A chill crept over her skin.

Understanding the sensation, Aimee ducked and avoided Knight's punch as it swung towards her. Staying low she kicked at the back of his knees and watched him drop to the floor. Standing up, she ripped off his sunglasses and clutched her PAVA spray. Exposed as they were, his eyes seemed to faintly glow, shimmering with the subtlety of a lake's surface on a moonless night. The abnormal beauty of this vision halted Aimee for a moment, mesmerising her with a nightmarish eloquence. Fighting through the hypnotic wonder, she quickly came to her senses and unleashed a dose of PAVA spray into his face. The liquid filled his eyes, burning them with a searing pain.

'This is for Andy Osborne, you bastard,' Aimee's anger dripped with a vengeful satisfaction.

Knight howled in pain as the cocktail of chemicals worked their effect, watched over by the grimacing Special Constable.

'And this is for Ollie, you piece of shit,' she screamed before kicking him in the face.

Teeth flew from his mouth as he fell backwards, landing on the angled legs of the upturned chair. Forrest seized the moment and ran at Knight, slamming a boot into his chest. The metal poles of the chair legs pierced his flesh and drove deep into his body amid agonizing screams. Not content, Aimee stamped on his torso again and again, slowly driving the chair legs, inch by inch, further into his body. The basement echoed with the sound of crunching bone as the chair legs cracked against the inside of his rib cage before tearing through his flesh and protruding out the other side.

The Special Constable wiped Knight's blood from her splattered brow as she watched his head slump to the side, lifelessly dangling from his neck.

'Got you, you fucker,' she yelled at the corpse, before letting the room fall into silence.

The air felt strangely thinner, the darkness free of the invisible terrors that had filled its crowded space. The only sound was that of Aimee, panting as she caught her breath.

The calm was fleeting, broken by the grotesque twisting of limbs, as slowly Knight's arms and legs began to contort; curling round at strange, jagged angles, like the legs of a dead spider. Forrest jumped back and watched as the corpse shrivelled and constricted in a chorus of snapping bone. Its skin stretched and pulled as the movements beneath the flesh flexed causing Knight's features to form broken shapes. Slowly the corpse writhed around the chair legs it was impaled on, bending and twisting, until eventually its limbs fell still, knotted and broken, leaving a sight so foul and unnatural it could no longer be described as human.

Shocked by the sight the Special constable edged backwards, feeling around the walls until she found the stairwell and made her way back to the ground floor. Reaching the top step, Aimee tried wiping his blood from her face, but her attempts resulted in smearing it further round her skin like some kind of barbaric war paint.

The craziness that took over Knight's corpse played on her mind, but it did nothing to dampen the fire of determination that burned in her stomach. Her battle in the dark with the crazed Knight had proved she was capable. Andy Osborne was right to have faith in her. Aimee was a cop, and a born fighter.

Making her way back outside, she squinted as her eyes adjusted to the daylight. The sun was hidden behind the overcast sky and although the day was darkening with the black clouds of a brooding storm, it was positively bright in comparison to the dark recesses of the blood filled basement she'd just emerged from.

Aimee had to get her brother and his friends to safety. She'd already broken her promise to PC Pritchard and done more than simply observe. There was no back up coming. And even if it did arrive, it would be too late.

Action needed to be taken urgently.

She needed a plan.

Crouching behind a large piece of sewage piping, yet to be laid, Aimee looked out over the construction site. At the centre of the large basin-like dip was the scene of the trade off, only it was empty.

Where had they gone?

Thunder rumbled overhead. It was getting louder. The storm was building; moving closer.

Her temple grew cold as the cool metal of a gun barrel was placed against her head.

TEN

Holding its broken chain delicately between her fingers, Kayleigh dangled her pendant in front of her eyes. Her crying had faded and her mind, as fragile as it felt, had calmed, pushing the emotional torment from the spotlight of her consciousness. Kayleigh knew the terrors were still there, she could feel the hole they had left in her thoughts, an impact crater so toxic she refused to fill it with anything else.

Cuddling her own legs in the front passenger seat of the police car she rested her head against her knees and watched the pendant gently spin. It looked like a silver drop, a precious teardrop, twisting as it fell from a light, summer breeze. Engraved across the liquid-like surface were intricate patterns that interlocked and double-backed, like a complex, confusing lattice. The smooth contours were sporadically broken by irregular, jagged spikes. The rise into these peaks seemed natural, as if the pendant had no other choice but to configure into its bizarre shape. Kayleigh smiled as she regarded the way it looked, its lines brought about a feeling of pleasure.

The chain had been snapped after it had been pulled from someone's neck, and could no longer be worn, but that was no bother to the seventeen year old, she'd get another chain. She had so many of them at home, ill-gotten rewards from her shoplifting activates. Kayleigh felt no guilt about her history of petty crime. If the shopkeepers insisted on making it so easy then it was up to her to teach them a lesson.

But she'd been so stupid this morning, making a grab at an open display in Meredith's the jewellers. It was a rushed snatch, nothing covert about it, and she certainly didn't check to see the coast was clear, otherwise she would have certainly seen the two police officers walking their beat.

Her dream had played on her mind, muddled her thoughts, but it was more the meeting of Ollie, the desire to impress him, that had egged her on to act so impulsively. She'd hoped they'd meet up with him and Jake when Eleanor had said she could hang out with her and Laura this morning.

That had gone to plan. Everything else hadn't.

The whole thing had been futile anyway. She'd dropped the necklace during the chase with the police and couldn't have embarrassed herself further in the face of the man she'd sought to impress. The sound of the shopkeeper screaming after her whilst he flagged down the officers still made her cheeks burn with shame.

The pendant in her hands now, was a spoil of more mysterious events and had come from somewhere in the tussle outside the bank. They'd nearly given the police the slip, but turning a corner onto Market Street, they collided into the corporately dressed group with the briefcase. They must have been mistaken for muggers as the confusion descended quickly into a wave of panic, fists and gunshots.

A van driver, Ollie's friend Sam, was waiting at the traffic lights on the same street and had called out to them. Her hands clawed at people, desperate to keep up and not be left behind as they all dived into his vehicle. It was then, as they sped off through the red light, she'd found the charm in the centre of her closed palm.

Kayleigh stared out the window of the police car and watched the angry clouds as they jostled for position overhead, creating a patchwork of blacks and greys. Their edges drifted on the wind, producing disturbing trails, like tendrils, that flailed around in the afternoon sky. The sun was slowly shrinking against the power of these dark, vapourous leviathans.

She watched the clouds twist and break, moving into new patterns against the influence of the wind. A flowing mane melted into creation as a cloud passed over one of the last few gaps of clear sky left in the celestial canopy. The mane was followed by an eye, then a nose, then a long, protruding horn. Kayleigh was momentarily mesmerised as a pair of rearing hooves broke free from the cloud, finally extinguishing the last rays of sunlight and casting unsettling darkness across the construction site and surrounding city.

The spectral unicorn snorted with fury as its eye glowed red, like the fire of a thousand burning grudges. It looked down at Kayleigh as the sky dissolved, evaporating into a void, eclipsed by the fiery orb that dominated the skyline. The gaze pulled at her soul, unravelling the binds that held her to this earthly plane. Her lungs scorched as the unblinking anger penetrated deeper, turning from fiery red to an all-consuming black and drowning her in flame.

Kayleigh screamed through fear and agony, breaking the vision and freeing the sky from the monstrous apparition.

She looked at the pendant in her hand. Its jagged edges suggested the shape of a mane, wild in the wind, leading to a great horn resting between two eyes.

'Are you okay?' PC Pritchard tapped on the window.

Kayleigh wound it down and tried to regain her composure as she looked at the Constable's friendly face.

'I'm fine, Officer,' she forced a smile.

'Please, call me Paul,' he smiled back and held the radio to his ear. 'I can't tell if I'm getting through or not.'

Paul tried again, speaking over waves of feedback and static in an attempt to signal for help. He held the radio close as he listened hard, trying to pick out voices in the dirge; searching for a sign they'd been heard.

'…fire reporte…medical…North street riot repor…lightning strikes o…'

Fragments of distress calls filtered through the interference, a barrage of voices littering the airwaves, each one with a desperate urgency in their tone.

'…please respond we need hel. . . armed response requi…'

As Kayleigh overheard the broken sentences rising and falling against the distortion, they momentarily sounded like the chanting of monks in prayer.

'It's chaos out there,' PC Pritchard muttered to himself.

Looking down at the eavesdropping teenager, he clocked the worried expression that creased her face.

'Don't worry,' he reassured her. 'They'll hear us real soon. Probably already have done and are on their way. Until then, how about we keep you safe. If you close the window I'll lock the car. Without this key no one's getting in.'

Kayleigh looked behind her to the back seat where Sergeant Byrne was still gently rocking, mouthing inaudible words whilst his eyes looked up at the ceiling.

'Don't worry about him,' Paul clocked her concerned expression. 'He can't get through the grid. That partition is just like a cage.'

Kayleigh smiled back in response and as Paul jangled the key in front of his face, she pressed the control on the inside of the door. As the window closed he pressed the button on the key, locking the doors and making her sanctuary complete. Paul's voice was muffled but still audible through the glass.

'You see? No one's getting in there. Even the windows are locked now,' he said with another comforting smile. 'I'll keep watch out here, okay? I'll stand guard and try the radio, all the while keeping my ear out for when the cavalry arrive.'

Paul walked a few metres away from the car, berating himself for letting Kayleigh hear those radio messages. Snippets of troubling scenarios from across the city had been steadily emerging through the white noise since he'd been wrestling to make contact. Even without the communication problems the police force would have been stretched, with them, well it was already pandemonium.

The concerned officer looked across the construction site. He was unable to see Forrest and thankful she had kept her surveillance covert. There was no need to take any rash action just yet, but how long did they really have?

PC Pritchard looked at the blackening sky and sighed, his hope for any help was fading fast.

Special Constable Forrest fell to the floor, her face slamming into the gravel and dried mud as she was thrown by her gun totting captor.

With the barrel of a Beretta handgun pointed at her head, Aimee had been marched back towards the entrance of the building she'd just left, where she was currently being exhibited like a trophy from a big game hunt. The hunter gave a little smirk of satisfaction, no doubt her expression of glee was much more telling behind her Jackie Ohh II Ray-Ban's. She pushed the point from one of her high heeled shoes into Aimee's back, forcing the Special Constable's face further into the dirt. White teeth began to gleam behind thick red lips as her smirk widened into a smile.

'Aimee!' Jake called out as he watched his sister being humiliated in front of them all.

She lifted her face out of the dirt and scowled at her brother.

'You've really fucked up this time, you little shit!'

she said, openly berating her brother. 'Why did you run? Didn't you see it was me?'

'I'm so sorry,' Jake's voice quivered; his head hung in shame.

Cross lifted her foot from Aimee's back, allowing her prisoner to straighten upright and kneel alongside their other captives.

Both Cross and Scullin had their guns trained on Aimee, Jake, Eleanor and Sam. Laura was beside them, her hands still tied and awkwardly carrying the briefcase. The Special Constable glanced over, her face screwing up with a mixture of disgust and anger as she clocked Sam's mangled hand.

'King, report,' Scullin ordered as his colleague emerged from the gloom of the dilapidated building.

'Knight is dead, sir,' King replied in military fashion.

'Sure is. So's the other gorilla you sent to get me,' Aimee spat in defiance.

'But where's the key?' Scullin asked his subordinate, his calm tone sounded strained with impatience. 'Knight and Duell had their duty, you do too. We need that second key.'

'I have not been able to find it,' King ground his teeth back and forth in anger, before snatching the briefcase from Laura's hands and knocking her to the ground. 'There was a corpse in one of the buildings,' King continued with his report. 'At least, bits of one. Knight had made quite a meal of the dissection. It was a male, that much I'm certain of.'

'Ollie! Oh my god!' Jake buried his face in his hands whilst the others turned white with the news of their friend's demise.

'I'm sorry, Jake,' from afar, Aimee could do nothing to comfort him.

'But no key amongst the mess,' King concluded.

'Then where is it?' Scullin cast his gaze, inquisitively across the youths that stood before him, eyeing them thoughtfully for a moment in silence.

He turned to face his team. Cross and King looked at him expectantly.

'Wasn't there another girl?'

'Yes sir,' King shouted through the growing wind, 'I believe there was.'

'She's the one,' Scullin's comment almost sounded like a question. 'She must be the one. I know it's somewhere close by. I can feel it. I can feel *her*. Somewhere in the wind.'

'I did not locate her on my reconnaissance,' King confirmed.

'But she's here. She's close. These cretins are of no use to us now, we'll hunt her down ourselves.' He gestured towards the captives, 'You may kill them at will.'

'Quickly?' Cross asked, with a tone of disappointment.

'However you wish,' Scullin casually remarked as he turned to walk back in the direction of the limousine.

Cross's evil grin widened with a gleeful malice on hearing her leader's command.

Jake closed his eyes as he felt King place a gun to the back of his head. Perhaps it was the cold touch of the steel barrel, or perhaps it was the anticipatory shock of what was to come that made his head grow heavy on his neck. A sudden numbness forced his thoughts to swim through a clouded consciousness.

A shot fired out causing his ears to ring with temporary tinnitus as he heard a thud on the ground next to him. Fearing for his friends, but powerless to help, he kept his eyelids sealed, awaiting his turn.

Shouts behind him erupted, and an unfamiliar voice cut through the din.

He opened his eyes, and as his vision cleared, he saw King nursing his own hand as it dripped with blood, almost black in the storm light.

Beside the wounded man, the briefcase lay on its side, metres from his feet, where he had released it in shock.

'Drop your guns,' the unfamiliar voice came again, clearer this time.

Jake followed the direction of sound to see a man in tan coloured chinos and a black roll-neck jumper holding a gun whose chamber was still emitting wisps of smoke. His thin moustache highlighted the scowl on his face as he surveyed the scene in front of him. Behind him stood two men whose bellies strained against their shirts, but their hulking biceps were evidence they were not strangers to the gym. They both gripped Uzi submachine guns and respectively held their aim on Scullin and Cross.

'I said drop your fucking guns!' the moustached man demanded. He nodded to the Uzis carried by his colleagues as he warned, 'These bad boys throw out enough lead per second to tear you to pieces.'

Scullin eyed the weapons, considering his next move, but finally acquiesced, throwing his gun to the floor. Even he would not be able to shrug off the hail of bullets they were able to unleash.

Following their leader, King and Cross did the same and tossed their weapons to the ground.

The gunman allowed himself a satisfied smile as he watched his opponents comply with his command.

'You thought you'd got away cleanly, huh? Not turning out to be your day,' he continued. 'You bastards stole something from us this morning. Grinch,' he tilted his head so as to direct his voice towards his companions behind him, 'keep those fuckers in your sights. If anyone so much as twitches, smoke the lot of them. Barry, get the case.'

ELEVEN

Sitting by the car, PC Pritchard reached into his pocket and pulled out a crushed packet of cigarettes. He placed one to his lips and savoured the moment as he lit the tip and took the first inhalation of much needed nicotine. It'd been a while since his last smoke, and he'd done well to cut down as much as he had, but a job like his was high stress, making it difficult to abstain completely.

Working as a cop he could always find a good excuse to light up.

Being unable to call for back up in the middle of a violent hostage situation when the rest of the city seemed to be going to shit as well seemed like as good excuse as any.

'Who are you?' Aimee asked the moustached man holding a Glock and barking orders.

He eyed her with a curious intensity as he smoothed his moustache with his index finger and thumb.

'Who the fuck am I, princess?' came the angry and hostile response. 'I'm Jonathan Bones. I'm the man who woke up this morning thinking today was all my birthday's rolled into one.' His face reddened as his words flowed from his mouth. 'I'm the man who after months of negotiation with some pain-in-the-ass mysterious stranger was going to be the owner of the most priceless and sought after object known to mankind.' Bones's voice strained under his anger, but still he spoke with an eloquence, ensuring each word was pronounced clearly, even if his speech had the subtly of a steamroller. 'But now I find myself stood in this fucking dust bowl, and worrying if I'm gonna get my chinos splashed with blood.

'Why do I find myself stood here?' His question was rhetorical, leaving no pause for anyone to answer. 'Because as I collect the combination to a safe deposit box, then head to the bank I've been told to go to in order to retrieve my treasure. *My* treasure, that I spent so long hunting for. That I spent so much of my own hard earned wealth on. As I pick it up from the safe deposit box of the city's most secure bank, *Mr Sunglasses* and his fucked up friends somehow manage to walk in and pull a heist.'

Lost in his rant, Jonathan Bones didn't see Scullin turn to King with a quizzical look.

'Can you find one?' he whispered.

'It is difficult without contact but I think there is a possibility,' King replied, his smile widening as he spoke. 'I can sense one whose heart is so dark, and they've already been exposed. It's almost like they were prepared for me.'

'Such is the way,' came Scullin's hushed and unsurprised affirmation.

'Perfect,' King replied, 'they'll be my puppet.'

Kayleigh smelt the plumes of cigarette smoke from outside the car. She smiled and wondered if she asked nicely, he'd let her have one.

'It's too late you know.'

A voice slithered from behind her, making her jump with a start.

She turned to see Sergeant Byrne looking directly at her, his manic panting soothed to an agitated state that was closer to calmness than she'd seen in him, but still far removed from serenity.

'It's too late. There's no point fighting it,' his breath smelt of stale coffee. She could taste the foul flavour as he spoke in the closed confines of the police car. 'I've seen it. You have to give in, you have to let go. There's no use fighting.'

Kayleigh leant back against the windscreen, trying to put as much distance between them. Despite the barred partition that kept him caged she felt unsafe; he unnerved her with his spasming ticks, wild eyes and oafish frame.

'You've no idea what's going on,' she retorted, unwilling to entertain the ravings of a mad man.

'I do. I really do. I know you're afraid. I know you're going to die. And I know there's something in *me*,' his ramblings grew hushed and increasingly sinister as spittle dribbled down his chiselled chin. He started to shake as he eyed the teenager. 'I can feel it.'

His fingers clenched the cage that separated them,

poking his fingertips through and reaching out towards her; shaking the metallic mesh as he tried to loosen it from its fittings.

Suddenly, he let out a shriek of pain.

'You've got to help me,' he cried, making a plea for help. 'You've got to-'

His words were cut short as the agony overwhelmed him. Kayleigh watched in shock as his arms bulged, inflating like balloons and splitting the fabric of his uniform as it strained against his increasing bulk. Byrne clenched his jaw as his skin flushed red with the rising blood that pumped below the surface of his skin. His veins popped out from his neck and pulsed like undulating fibres. Kayleigh went for the door, but it was locked. In panic she looked around for the central locking system, but the workings of a car, especially a police car, were foreign to her.

Byrne's hands began to swell, filling the holes of the mesh he'd pushed his fingers through. They continued growing, the grating cutting into the skin until the ends of his fingers were severed from the pressure, dropping off and revealing gnarled, claw-like bone. His neck continued to bulge, and grew out like a croaking frog as his veins turned black, filling his skin with a patchwork of midnight shades. He opened his mouth, which gapped unnaturally wide, releasing a two foot tongue that felt its way across the buckling cage, leaving a slimy trail of salvia in its wake. Amidst a strange, tormented, gargling sound, the officer's torso inflated, filling the back of the police car as Kayleigh banged on the window for help, desperate to alert PC Pritchard.

Paul stood up and turned in time to see the back

passenger window shatter. An arm, four times its normal length, smashed through the glass and caught the PC on his shoulder. Its bony digits dug into his flesh like talons. He fell forwards as the thing that was Sergeant Byrne ripped through the body of the patrol car, tearing it in two.

Free from its captivity the monster stood ten feet high on all fours like some bloated, malformed gazelle. Its body puffed and deflated with the rise and fall of its laboured breaths whilst a congealed, sweaty substance slipped from skin that looked diseased in its colouring and paper thinness.

It crouched down to eye Kayleigh as she sat, trapped in the front half of the police car. Torn from the rest of the vehicle, the driver's compartment still had the caged fencing, giving it some form of protection against the monster as its greedy eyes, still very much Byrne's, studied her with a hunger. How long these defences would last was only a matter of time.

'Over here you ugly fucker,' PC Pritchard shouted.

The monster turned towards him, its bulbous head housing a mouth that looked more like a ragged tear across its face. A large tongue hung from the ugly slit, drooling with an unknown need whilst needle-like teeth poked out at awkward angles as if they'd been crammed in by an overzealous creator.

Opening its lethal maw, it unleashed a ferocious but broken sound, a disturbing aural cocktail of a roar from a grizzly bear and something akin to the grinding of metal, before launching itself towards the Police Constable.

Bounding with surprising speed on its sinewy limbs,

it galloped after its prey. Paul turned and ran but the monster was on him in moments, capturing him in one of its large hands and pinning him to the ground.

Kayleigh tried to escape from the wreckage of the car, but what was once her protection had become her prison. The crushed metal had folded in, sealing the doors shut, despite her efforts to force them open.

She watched the monster run its tongue over PC Pritchard's face before sinking its teeth into his already wounded shoulder, biting hard into the flesh and pulling back, slowly tearing his arm from his torso in jagged, jerky movements. He called out, begging for help as the thing that was once Sergeant Byrne chewed on his bicep and crunched through his bones.

The monster lowered its head again to take another bite. This time Kayleigh looked away. Paul's screams were so primal, so raw in their terror, they echoed through the girl's very core. She dived to the floor of the car, hiding in the foot well, and tried to block out the sounds. Noises of tearing and crunching pounded her ears, mixed with the sickening sound of liquid splashing like heavy rain. It was as if the storm had finally broken, but the teeth-grinding tension remained ample in the atmosphere of terror.

'Fuck knows how they did it,' Jonathan Bones continued his diatribe as Barry made his ungainly way towards the case. 'But there I am, making my withdrawal, and bang, *Nobody move*. They take what's mine, lock it in their own briefcase and leave.'

Grinch aimed his gun at Cross with exaggerated movements, untrusting of the violence that emanated from her expression.

Bones glanced over and smiled, then turned his attention to Jake and his friends. 'I've got to say thanks to you little shits for running into them just as they left the bank. You knocked them flying!' He laughed with enforced enthusiasm. 'I have to admit I think they over reacted,' his laughter faded as he wiped the remains of his mirth from his water filled eyes. 'Must have thought you were part of my gang. That or just someone else that wanted what's in *there*,' he motioned his gun towards the briefcase. 'There isn't a person on this planet that wouldn't, if they knew it existed.'

Bones trailed of for a moment, lost in a day dream of wonder; a private reverie that had him momentarily spellbound.

He quickly snapped back to reality.

'But like I said, thanks to you kids for stalling them. Gave us time to get our shit together and start tracking them. Fuck me, you weren't too hard to find.' Jonathan looked towards Scullin and his cronies. 'Just had to follow the trail of destruction. You lot sure make a mess,' he chuckled at his own comment. 'My girlfriend says I talk too much. Do I talk too mu-?'

An unearthly roar halted the gunman's rant followed by the far off screams of a dying man.

'What the fuck is that?' Jonathan ducked; an instinctive reflex to the barrage of sounds. 'Barry, grab the case.'

Barry leant forward and picked up the briefcase, huffing and puffing as he straightened himself back up.

'Coming boss,' he called back.

'Something's coming alright,' King muttered to

himself.

'What are you smiling at?' Jonathan directed his question to King. 'You want me to shoot you again?'

His question went unanswered as a deafening screech cut through the air. The thumping sound of galloping feet shook the ground and everyone turned in time to see Barry drop the case, spasming in shock as a long, bony appendage sliced into his back and out through his chest. The monstrous form of the misshapen Sergeant Byrne knocked him to the ground as it landed beside him, then lifted his still quivering body. Placing the back of Barry's head into its razor filled mouth, it crunched into the bone, splitting the man's skull amidst a spray of brain matter that exploded from the force like pink confetti.

It reached out a long arm and grasped Eleanor before she had time to react. Holding her with one hand it walked on its remaining three limbs, rearing to slash its free claw at the others.

She struggled in its grip, but Eleanor was unable to prise herself free from the vice-like hold of its sinewy, sweat drenched digits.

'What the fuck is that?' Jonathan cried as he staggered back in disbelief, aiming his gun toward the demonic shape that gnashed its teeth towards him.

Sam raced towards Cross's discarded gun and picked it up. Lining the sight he fired it towards the monster.

'Take that you bastard!' he shouted at the nightmare made real.

But with his dominant hand crushed beyond use, his shot fired off target. King gripped him by the neck and held him prone, allowing the dark puppet to do as its master commanded and slice through Sam's torso. It wasn't a clean cut, and as Sam's top half fell to the floor, the weight of his bulk snapped his spine with a splintering crack.

Opening her eyes for the briefest of moments, Kayleigh caught sight of PC Pritchard's dark crimson blood. The car's windows on the left hand side had been drenched with the scarlet liquid. Unidentifiable pieces of flesh and jagged rips of skin slowly ran along the glass, following the slow current of the viscous blood.

The terrified girl closed her eyes tightly again, wishing for it all to go away. She wished she was back in her bed. But last night even her sleep had provided little comfort.

Outside, the tearing, the screaming, the sickening sound of cracking had all been silenced with the crescendo of a hideous squeal. A barely describable noise, whose memory lingered in Kayleigh's ears.

She gripped her pendant tightly in her fist and felt the raised spikes that dotted the surface dig into her hand. Continuing to squeeze, she dared the piece of jewellery to cut her, to tear at her flesh. Kayleigh savoured the pain that grew in her palm, forcing it to build until her hand turned wet from the cuts that bled; leaking through her fingers and offering a strange climax that left her momentarily breathless.

The pendant had not been hers for very long, only a matter of hours. She'd acquired it accidentally, but somehow it felt right that it was in her possession. As small as it was, the silver charm was the only ray of positivity that had come from today, and Kayleigh clung to it desperately.

Looking through the red tinged window she saw the glow of Paul's cigarette still burning on the ground. Stupidly she felt herself yearn for its hit. Her eyes caught something moving in the dirt; long and dark, weaving across the sun-baked mud like a snake. It didn't take her long to realise it wasn't an animal at all, but a trail of liquid; petrol to be exact, leaking from the split tank of the patrol car. The smell confirmed her fears and as she noticed the puddle that surrounded her had reached out with many tendrils, one of those tentacles met with the burning cherry of the half smoked Marlboro.

Jake ran to Laura as she stared transfixed at the events in front of her.

'Come on, let's go,' he said as he tried and failed to pull her to her feet.

Aimee dived for Barry's fallen Uzi, but was intercepted by the thrashing limbs of the monster. Catching her leg, it threw her against the wall of a crumbling building. She stood up to catch her breath and saw the man named Grinch offload a number of rounds. They shot wildly into the air, but the spray managed to catch its bestial hide. It roared with pain but responded quickly, thrusting its claw through Grinch's bloated stomach.

'Cross, get the case,' Scullin commanded his subordinate, unsure of the supernatural animal that reared before him.

'I can't,' she replied with venom. 'It's under the hell spawn.'

'King,' Scullin snapped, 'move your monster.'

'It's not that easy,' sweat ran down his brow, as the physical attrition of his activities began to take their toll. 'This one's so wild I'm barely holding on.'

The monster turned its attention back to Eleanor and began to sink its demonic bite into the soft flesh of her side. Eleanor twisted in its grip, managing to pull herself away from the lethal radius of its over-sized jaws. Only succeeding in tearing an inch of meat from her torso, it dragged her towards its open mouth once more, determined to taste her death.

A burst of gunfire filled the air. The monster dropped the wounded girl and turned to its attacker, its limbs already unstable beneath it. Another burst of gunfire sounded out, this time hitting its mark more clearly. The monster's front left gave way and it fell to the ground.

It lashed out with its right arm, catching its attacker and causing Bones to drop his Glock as it wrapped him in its limb. Unable to stand, the creature snapped its vicious mouth like a beached fish and pulled him across the dirt towards its jagged teeth. With his hand scrabbling for grip, Bones reached out and caught Grinch's dropped Uzi. Aiming it at the flailing monster he waited until they could almost touch, until he could smell the rotting odour from the mucus on its skin before pulling the trigger.

'Die you motherfucker!' Jonathan screamed as he unleashed round after round from his deceased colleague's submachine gun.

The artillery filled the creature's head, ripping flesh and bone like it was nothing more substantial than tissue paper. Blood as black as ink sprayed from the thing as its grotesque features were destroyed by a torrent of bullets.

King cursed as the smoking barrel was turned and trained on him.

'What the fuck was that?' Jonathan Bones cried, climbing back to his feet. 'In fact, don't tell me. I don't want to know. Damn it. I knew I'd get messed up in some weird shit if I pursued this.' He stopped his monologue and turned his attention back to his captives, 'All too busy trying to save each other that none of you made a run for it. You sure are dumb.'

Scullin had been edging closer to the neglected briefcase that lay near the creature's corpse, but froze as Jonathan's gun barrel aimed towards him.

'Get away from that case, Mr Sunglasses,' he threatened. 'You're just too slow aren't you?' He wiped sweat from his eyes as he took a moment to breathe; a futile attempt to calm himself. 'Nobody move. Nobody move a fucking muscle. All... *this*,' he waved his free hand in the direction of the fallen monster and his slain bodyguards, unable to fittingly describe the carnage surrounding him, 'has made me a little twitchy right now and I swear I'll fill you all full of holes if anybody even sneezes. That includes you, little Miss Police.' He turned his gun on Aimee and motioned for her to kneel down.

He smiled as she complied.

'That's better,' came a satisfied tone.

Eleanor's side throbbed as it trickled blood, staining her summer dress that already stuck to her skin through a mixture of sweat and the watery slime the creature had been secreting. The discomfort of her injury was a minor irritation compared to the screaming fears that filled her head as she stared at the ravaged meat of Sam's severed corpse.

Just beyond her reach lay Scullin's Berretta. She felt vengeance fill her heart, not drowning out her anguish but complimenting it; sweetening it to a palatable taste. Although coolly composed on the outside, fires raged behind her serenity.

Jonathan's eyes scanned from one person to the next, with his weapon following suit, as he carefully made his way to the discarded briefcase.

As the flames took hold and travelled down the liquid pathway, back to her prison, Kayleigh kicked at the doors and shouldered against the caged partition. All held resolutely against her attempts of escape.

The fiery line crackled as it burnt, a sound like far away hooves galloping ever closer. Hypnotised by the destructive beauty of the oncoming flames, Kayleigh gave up her futile escape and watched as they danced along the ground like sprites from old fashioned fairy tales. Faces flickered amongst the orange glow with wicked smiles and hellish red eyes that taunted and teased her with their lethal presence.

Noises pricked her ears. But these weren't the strange animal-like sounds that came from PC Pritchard's attacker, nor were they the low roar of an advancing fire. These had a human quality, their pitch rising and falling to the sound of human syllables. Kayleigh couldn't decipher any words, but the sound was incessant and rhythmic, like the sound of chanting.

As the chorus grew louder, Kayleigh watched four figures slowly walk towards her. They were dressed in flowing robes; frayed and dirty; the garments had seen better days but the coloured patterns of yellow and blue on grey were striking in the threatening dark of the building storm.

The figures became clearer as they drew closer, and she was able to see that each one carried a staff the height of its owner, with fluid, beautiful markings carved into the wood. Their faces were painted with gold and blue patterns, matching the designs of their tattered robes. As intricate as the painted decoration was it did little to hide the horrific scarring that marked the face of one of their troupe.

Their chanting continued, as they surrounded the car; their drone growing louder and clearer through the glass. As the wind shook harder against the vehicle it carried their chorus on the breeze. The unknown words caressed Kayleigh's ears, gently kissing her worried thoughts and momentarily easing her mind.

When she looked back toward the fire, the flames had gone. Presumably extinguished by the atmospheric currents.

With the fading light, Kayleigh was just able to view the scarred man's companions. The others were not so horrifying, but their striking differences in appearance, from race, age, gender and build made them all just as strange for being together.

The procession had been led by a small, Indian man. He was barely five foot in height, with a hairless head and thin, withering frame. As he continued to mouth his religious chorus, Kayleigh could see crooked teeth dotting a near barren gum line. Juxtaposed to this shrivelled frame of a man stood a giant by comparison.

His shoulders were broad and his features could have been carved from an artist's dream of perfection. The expression he wore however, was battle-worn, and he looked ready for another fight. The woman appeared much younger than her companions, and even with her hair wrapped in a scarf and her face streaked with paint, the soft contours of her beauty were clear to see.

They ceased their chanting abruptly, and with the strangely dressed group now stood in silence, Kayleigh watched as the shrivelled, old man looked down at where the mangled limbs of PC Pritchard were scattered. He held his hands up, contorting his fingers into a strange configuration. His digits interlocked to produce a shape, unfamiliar to his captive, teenage audience.

They all closed their eyes, leaving only the sound of the wind to rise and fall like an invisible tide. A moment passed in this way, with everything but the breeze frozen. Even the background blur of the city traffic and screaming sirens had ceased, seemingly in respect for the ceremony taking place. Kayleigh wasn't able to say exactly when the chanting started again, but slowly it began to build, fading in from the silence as if carried on gentle gales from some far off land.

The cultists opened their eyes, then, following the direction of their leader, closed in on the car.

Kayleigh squeezed the pendent tight and sunk back into the seat. Unsure of their motives, she prayed they hadn't seen her.

'Now, if you don't mind,' Jonathan spoke with an even more heightened sense of agitation as he waved the Uzi in his sweaty palm, 'I'm just going to take what's mine and be off.'

Stopping by the case he bent his knees, lowering his free hand to reach the handle.

A smile filled his expression as he gripped it, almost daring to laugh with joy. But quickly that turned to a troubled look of concern and confusion.

Something wasn't right.

Clutching his stomach, he doubled over in pain, then righted himself, trying to find some composure whilst fighting against the discomfort that worked its way through him. He dropped his gun and pulled at his clothes, lifting his jumper to understand the burning feeling underneath; the growing agony that stung like electrified barbs. His enforced audience looked as horrified as him as they watched his skin pull apart; tearing itself from his torso. Cuts appeared like a haphazard lattice as wounds crawled across his body. The gashes grew further, deeper, past the skin and into the flesh. Tearing and pulling and ripping through him, this unnatural pox of self-destruction split muscle and snapped tendons. He watched as his intestines fell from a growing hole in his belly, coiling on the floor like a gore soaked snake. His stomach was to follow, slopping onto the ground like a water filled balloon, leaking its slushy contents as it burst onto his shoes. Unable to stand any further, Jonathan Bones dropped to his knees as his throat opened up and the flesh on his face crawled from his cheeks, wrenching itself into small chunks like a swarm of marauding cockroaches.

As the gunman's scream withered, Scullin looked to his colleagues, but they offered him the same quizzical expression in return.

'I don't understand,' King voiced their thoughts. 'If that wasn't us…'

'Rare for a Stygian to be out of answers,' came an ancient and unfamiliar voice. 'Maybe we can offer some assistance.'

Before them stood four figures in tattered robes; one woman and three men. The bold words, sounding like a threat, had come from the smallest of them, Taal, a withered looking man with the bluster of a thousand battles in his eyes. His stare looked deep into his opponents. Beside them stood Kayleigh.

A bead of sweat rolled down Scullin's temple.

TWELVE

Overpowered by Taal's unlikely strength, Kayleigh was pulled towards him as he forcibly grabbed her by the wrist. She struggled in his grip, trying to fight him off, but was unable to break free or resist the might with which he drew her close. The old man possessed more might than his time-ravaged, skeletal frame suggested.

'We almost missed this one's importance,' Taal spoke through dry, cracked lips as he eyed the girl squirming in his hold.

'Get off me,' Kayleigh protested, but was unable to prevent him from prising open her clenched fist.

In her palm was a smooth yet spikey piece of silver. Scullin leaned closer, eyeing the object.

'Interesting piece of jewellery, don't you think?' Taal spoke with a knowing tone, bordering on sarcasm.

His meaning was not lost on his adversary.

'I wasn't aware your faction believed in a sense of humour,' Scullin mocked.

'I didn't know your type were able to recognise it,'

came Taal's curt reply. 'We haven't met, personally, but I'm sure you know who I am,' he spoke to the large, suited man as he tossed Kayleigh towards his own group and into the arms of his giant-like colleague, Sanay. 'I know *what* you are. That's good enough for me.'

Special Constable Forrest rose to her feet with a puzzled expression on her face.

'Who the hell are you guys?' she asked, gesturing an incredulous wave towards the monk-like quartet.

'We are quite the contrary,' came a reply from the scarred Kal. His voice was refined and soft as it sailed on the breeze, a contrast to his fierce, wounded face.

'We are Servants of the Sacred Whisper,' Maja explained, thrusting her staff into the ground as she announced her proud proclamation.

Scullin took a step towards the robed figure. 'Give me the key.'

'Give me the case,' Taal challenged, mimicking his opponent's movement and shortening the distance between them. 'Its contents don't belong to you.'

'And yet we have it,' Scullin's knuckles cracked as he squeezed his fists in a deliberate sign of aggression.

Taal raised his staff and took up a fighting stance. Behind him, Kal, Maja and Sanay did the same.

'Then we must settle the matter your way,' the frail looking man threatened as fire burnt in his eyes.

He lunged forward, throwing himself at Scullin. Cross scooped up her gun from the dirt and took aim, shooting at the old man. With lightning quick reactions, Taal twisted in the air, spinning his body with the control of a gymnast and dodging the bullet. Landing on his feet he waved his staff above his head and whispered into the wind. Cross dropped her gun like is was scalding to the touch.

With all eyes elsewhere, Eleanor took her chance and ran towards Scullin's discarded Beretta, eager to take the gun and avenge Sam's death.

Grasping the handle she tried to lift the firearm but failed to raise it off the ground. She strained and grunted as she exerted every muscle in her body, but it wouldn't budge. She pulled at it again, feeling her back tearing under the skin as she tried.

How much did this thing weigh?

Looking over she watched others struggle with the same problem.

Had Taal done something to their weapons?

Distracted with the gun, she didn't notice Cross approach her from behind until slender fingers had wrapped around her throat and began to squeeze. Eleanor tried to fight back, but was too late, as quickly her strength evaporated. Within a matter of seconds Cross's powerful grip had crushed her windpipe. Another moment more and the stunned audience heard the sound of bones snapping as her spinal cord crunched between her attacker's palms. Trying to gasp for air, Eleanor could do nothing as Cross pulled at her neck, tearing the skin between her shoulders and head. Cross's fingers ripped through Eleanor's flesh as it split apart like worn cloth. Pulling her decapitated head free from her body, Cross held the teenager's severed cranium aloft. Blood poured down the arms of the savage murderer as the remnants of the girl's spine swayed in the wind.

Cross cried an ungodly scream and thunder

exploded in the sky above them.

The two warring groups charged at each other underneath a surge of lightning bolts that flashed overhead. Cross launched herself at Sanay, holding her hands out like talons. Taking his staff, he thrust it forward, driving the end into her face. It snapped her sunglasses in two and continued, driving through her eye socket and forcing through her brain until it thudded against the back of her skull. Cross howled and shook violently as Sanay lifted her on his staff, suspending the wounded woman high in the air. Her arms thrashed wildly in an instinctive bid to reach him, but failed. Abruptly her attempted attack halted as her limbs began to shrivel and curl in on themselves. Her corpse slowly twisted round his staff like a dying snake meekly constricting its final prey.

Sanay smiled, but his victory was soon quashed as he turned to see Cross stood in front of him, free from injury and smirking with a devilish grin.

'Confused?' she laughed as Scullin's titanic fist smashed through Sanay's skull, obliterating his head in a fountain of blood and bone.

'That's not right,' Aimee was momentarily taken aback by the unnatural sights that played out before her. Quickly she snapped back from her perplexed meanderings. 'Run for it!' she screamed to Jake, Laura and Kayleigh.

Like stunned rabbits the young trio had been mesmerised by the violent proceedings happening around them. Aimee's call to flee ignited the adrenalin in their legs and, using the distraction of the fight, they broke free from their captors and ran in all directions.

Scullin reached out to grab Kayleigh but was blocked by a blow from the staff of Taal.

'Get her,' Scullin shouted to Cross and King as he battled Taal in a duel between fist and weapon.

Hands swiped at Kayleigh, but clenching the key she found more speed and broke free. A pulse of energy seemed to throb from the metallic object, giving her renewed strength. She held the charm close to her chest while her legs carried her with a speed she did not think possible. Desperately searching for cover she found herself running towards a deserted building. Its walls bowed and deep cracks danced up the time-ravaged brickwork. But the building's near collapse didn't concern her, hiding did, and as she ran through the crumbling entrance she found herself lost in a world of shadows.

THIRTEEN

Following Kayleigh, Aimee gave chase, and watched as both Cross and King ran into the building where the seventeen year old had sought sanctuary. An old sign on the side of the building swung back and forth in the wind. Though scratched and faded, the words *Bus Depot* could still be read on its battered surface. Entering the building herself, Aimee stopped as her eyes tried to adjust to the darkness inside.

Hazy as it was, her vision began to make out objects in the gloom. Outlines and shapes emerged, revealing a huge, open expanse, so wide she could not see the far end; its detail consumed by the blackness. Metal staircases to both her left and right ascended to a walkway that followed the perimeter of the room. The overhang of this elevated pathway obstructed the view of the walls underneath it, casting shadows and blocking what little of the eerie storm tinged rays found its way through the filthy skylight; itself nothing more than a sliver of dull illumination projecting a glow of faint greens and browns from the ceiling.

From what visibility she had the room looked still, draped in an unquietening silence.

That silence was broken by the arrival of Maja and Kal. The gold from their ragged robes glinting in the darkness of the building, somehow finding a luminosity from even the smallest traces of light.

'Who the hell are you?' Aimee, turned around and whispered a threat, holding her fists up in a sign she was ready to fight.

'We are not your enemy,' Maja's voice was calm and soothing. 'We are here to help.'

'We want to save your friend from the others. She has something they should not possess,' Kal explained, placing a friendly hand on Aimee's shoulder. 'My name is Kal, and this is Maja. Please, you can trust us.'

Forrest had no knowledge of this strange group, but of the two sides they had seemed the least aggressive in their insanity. Kal's touch sent a wave of reassurance through her. Aimee smiled in a sign of acceptance and gently squeezed Kal's hand.

'Well, at least we want the same thing,' Aimee spoke softly.

Slowly the three edged forward with careful steps. Maja and Kal scanned the surrounding gloom like eagles in search of prey.

'Keep away from the shadows,' Maja warned the Special Constable as she strayed closer to the edges of the depot. 'The further into the darkness you go, the more dangerous they will be. Stay close.'

'Who are *they*?' Aimee asked as she got closer to

their huddle. 'Who are these *others*?'

'They are darkness,' Kal explained, his legion of scars exaggerated in the half-light.

'They are the Stygian, the Dark Guard,' Maja cut in. 'They are at one with the darkness, not just physically, but spiritually too. The laws of nature twist and bend around their foul presence.'

'Are they human?' Aimee asked, remembering Knight's eyes and the way his body buckled in death.

'Maybe. Once,' came Maja's disconcerting reply.

'Our great master Taal knows more than we,' Kal explained. 'We heard the call, Taal saw the vision. We had no choice. We had to leave our place of worship and come. Seek out the riches that had fallen in the wrong hands.'

'What are these riches? This treasure? What's in the briefcase that's got everyone so worked up?' Aimee whispered. 'Money? Diamonds? Gold?'

'There are things far more valuable than money,' Kal answered. 'Somethings have a wealth you could not conceive.'

'Then what?' Amiee asked, growing annoyed.

'A dark time approaches, Aimee Forrest,' Maja answered. 'The Stygian refer to it as *the Calling*, a time when their original masters grow closest to this existence. The contents of that briefcase contains something very special. Something that can bring the most delirious joy, but in the wrong hands it could unleash beings of unimaginable power; creatures even we cannot stop. The Calling begins today, and if they are successful, if these demons are released, it would bring about an age of destruction and suffering, the likes of which you have never seen.'

Aimee tried to laugh off the story, but the conviction in Maja's face, convinced her of something, though she didn't know what.

'Then why is it just left out there?' The Special Constable motioned to where they'd come from. Looking back through the open doorway they could just make out Scullin and Taal trading blows in the distance, whilst next to them the briefcase leant on its side, propped up by a chunk of disregarded plaster, and ignored by all.

'It is safe,' Kal replied.

Aimee looked back at him incredulously, 'It doesn't *look* safe.'

'It's safe,' his reassurance sounded smug in its confidence.

'It's not safe,' Maja whispered, cutting back in to the conversation, but still searching the shadows with her eyes as they kept their steady pace into the depths of the old depot. 'It's dangerous. Don't go anywhere near it, for your own sake. You saw what happened to the man that tried earlier. Taal cast the Eolhx to guard it. It's still out there.'

'The what?' Aimee asked, growing frustrated with the riddles.

'The Eolhx. It is a word,' Kal answered. 'It protects.'

'Why not set it on this *Dark Guard*?' Aimee was barely keeping up with the thread but probed for answers, looking for a way to end this already out of hand scenario.

'Eolhx does not attack. It protects. It can be

nothing else.'

'I thought you said it was a word?' Aimee grew more confused.

Maja took her by the shoulders and looked her in her eyes. 'There are sounds with meanings that go beyond your understanding of language. Scared syllables with powers that you can only begin to imagine. There are words that can kill, words that protect and words that can call across dimensions. The Servitude guards these secrets as we serve the sacred whispers on the wind. And they've been calling us here. Drawing us to you.'

Aimee tried to absorb what she'd been told, but there was no time to seek clarity. From out of the darkness came King, charging at the group with a swift speed. His fist struck Aimee and knocked her to the floor. Kal swung his staff but missed the man in the light grey suit. By the time Forrest got to her feet, King was out of sight.

'Stay close,' Maja commanded as they huddled together, back to back.

A scream-like cackle screeched through the building like the sound of a motor accident with a bus full of school kids. The terrifying noise was followed by King's face, a vision of twisted hatred, as it thrust out of the gloom once more. He dodged Kal's staff as it swung for his head and countered with a powerful punch that sent his would-be attacker flying backwards. By the time Aimee turned to help her new found colleague, King had caught hold of the Special Constable and, with impressive strength, lifted her above him. Maja turned and thrust her staff into the back of King's knee, making him fall to the floor and drop Aimee to the ground.

Quickly, he turned and swung a punch. Maja blocked it with her staff, pivoting the other end round to strike him across the face. King's sunglasses fell to the floor as he staggered sideways from the blow.

Another swipe caught the suited aggressor below the ribs, but before she had a chance to pull her staff back round, King took hold of Maja's weapon. He pulled it from her hands and tossed it behind him. It landed on the ground and rolled out of sight, disappearing into the dark. The next blow connected hard, sending Maja crashing to the floor. She lay unconscious as King approached her; defenceless against his brutish power.

Aimee ran towards him and jumped on his back. Linking her arms around his chest and clasping her hands together she arched backwards, trying to topple his balance and pull him over. King stumbled as he failed to find a steady footing and fell, taken by the force of the Special Constable.

Aimee landed in the darkness, but felt King slide from her grip, seemingly dissolving in her clutches. She caught her breath as she got to her feet and looked for her comrades. All around her was nothing but black. The dim illumination of the skylight had disappeared leaving a consuming darkness so impenetrable she could no longer see the unconscious bodies of Kal or Maja.

King's voice floated through the air. 'Where am I, Special Constable Forrest?' he taunted Aimee, his face unseen in the inky shadows. 'Where are *you*? Things looking a little different?'

'Where are you, you fucker? Where's Kayleigh?' she

demanded, shouting in the direction of the voice. 'What have you done with my friends?'

A sound of laughter crept in her ears, sending chills through her body. There was something familiar about the sound, something frightening. The last time she heard that laughter was this morning when she'd shared a joke with her colleague on the beat. She'd told a joke, an awful one at that, but she knew the policeman she admired had a taste for truly terrible punchlines. His laughter had been a thrill to her then, now it was awful and out of place.

A smile flashed through the darkness. The closer it grew the clearer it became until she could see the detail of a cracked tooth.

'You killed me, Forrest,' the voice of PC Andy Osborne spat from the mouth. An ashen white face, distorted with death and splashed with blood, looked at her with angry, sunken eyes. 'You let me die. You let them *all* die.'

Firelight softly licked at the darkness, revealing the outline of a row of headstones. Between the graves, worms writhed on the ground, creating a moving carpet of flesh that slithered in the shadows.

'I'm so sorry,' Aimee meekly protested, terrified of the view before her.

He smiled with a measured cruelty as he took hold of her wrists. His grin widened, growing in size until the skin at the corners of his mouth began to tear. The rips through his flesh continued, spreading across his face like a cracking piece of china, shredding his features into strips of skin that unravelled before Aimee's startled eyes.

His head collapsed into a mess of fleshy strands that blew on an unseen breeze like the tentacles from some underwater nightmare. Blood flew into the air as his body continued to undo, splashing onto Aimee's hands and burning cold, the instant it made contact.

She pulled away from his grip and watched what was left of her deceased colleague unwind; eventually collapsing at her feet in a whirl of human entrails, leaving nothing more than a pile of clothes and tendrils of flesh.

Stepping back in disgust she looked down at her hands as the blood burnt a chilling cold, deep into her fingers. Horrified, she watched as her palms slowly faded from view. Her arms were next as they too began to lose their visibility, the blackness creeping across her body.

As it spread to her chest she felt a pressure begin to crush her ribs, forcing the air from her lungs. She fought for breath as she wrestled with the darkness, trying to fight it as it spread across her body.

A hand caught her collar and pulled Aimee backwards, freeing her from the grip of the shadows. Landing hard on the floor she was relieved to be back under the murky glow of the skylight, her arms and hands visible once more, and the freezing pain dissipating.

A flash of gold caught her attention and she saw her saviour, Kal, stood half in the shadows cast by the elevated walkway. He seemed to be struggling with an attacker, someone unseen. The darkness danced strangely on his body, like it was writhing with its own will, wrapping itself around the brave monk-like figure like a living oil slick.

Kal wailed in agony and turned to Aimee, holding his hand out to her. Aimee tried to get to her feet but was stopped by Maja who knelt beside her.

'You can't help him now,' the young woman in the headdress warned. 'Their world is one of cruelty and madness. I pity what visions he made you endure.'

Stunned at the sight she was witnessing, Aimee watched as Kal was pulled into the dark. The shadows engulfed him completely, stifling his screams amid the crunch of snapping bone. He forced himself out from the black for a moment, his face swelling and twisted whilst tusk-like teeth forced their way through his cheeks. Kal unleashed a bestial cry before being swamped once more by the darkness. Blood poured from the black where he once stood and flooded the floor that surrounded the shocked Special Constable.

'What was that?' Aimee asked.

'Each of the Dark Guard has a unique way in which their powers manifest. King controls matter and minds. He created that hell spawn you fought earlier, the one that killed your colleague. It looks like he was trying a similar trick with Kal.

'Some twist senses, some can mimic other's form, cast illusions or show brutish strength and durability. Did you see watch Cross die at the hands of Sanay, then appear before him? Their powers are varied, but all of them are deadly,' Maja said, her eyes transfixed on the darkness in front of them.

King stepped back into the half-light, his footsteps splashing in the blood that soaked the floor. A grin spread across his face, growing underneath his uncovered eyes that, now exposed, looked like two large, black holes, filling his face from nose to temple. Aimee shuddered to look at them; like twin pits of evil. He circled the two women that crouched on the floor in the centre of the building, his words echoing in the vast expanse.

'This has been a very troubling day,' he sneered. 'But your friend tasted good. Will you be the same?'

Maja charged at him with her weapon held high. The two collided, staff to fist; both held their ground.

'Your kind talk a lot don't you?' Maja mocked as she swung again.

King blocked the attack to his side but was defenceless against the second as she swept the staff under him, taking his legs out and knocking him to the floor. Thrusting her weapon downwards, she drove its end into his stomach, tearing through his shirt and piercing his flesh. King howled with agony whilst his assailant called out a sentence of incomprehensible sounds.

A draught began to sweep through the old bus depot, building in force the louder and longer Maja chanted.

His head throbbed from the incantation, but gritting his teeth through the pain that gripped his body, King took hold of the staff that impaled him and, with both hands, snapped the weapon in two. Maja dived out of his reach as he stood up, still with half the staff protruding from his stomach. He threw the other half. Its end, sharp from the break, sliced into Maja's side as she tried unsuccessfully to avoid his aim. She fell on her hands and knees, clutching her wound and groaning in pain. King staggered towards her as blood spurted in torrents from his injured body. His limbs twitched in jerky, violent movements as he drew closer.

A figure appeared at the edge of the room, a girl, briefly emerging from the darkness, before disappearing again.

'Kayleigh!' Aimee called out to the face she recognised.

King stood over Maja, her back to him, and watched as she clutched the bloody hole in her side. He said nothing, but wobbled precariously on his feet as he observed her suffering. Aimee ran towards them but was unable to stop King as he fell forward onto the robed woman. The broken staff that protruded from his stomach drove into Maja's back, tearing through her torso and forced through her body by the weight of the man in the light grey suit. The two collapsed together on the floor and rolled onto their sides like a pair of post-coital lovers. Maja looked towards Aimee and gripped the end of the staff, trying in vain to pull herself free from the broken pole that speared both her and King. She felt his faint breath on her ear, but as his breathing slowly faded, King's limbs buckled and twisted. His bones cracked and tendons snapped as his arms and legs curled in on themselves with the manner of a dying insect, wrapping around Maja as she struggled to hold on to life.

'Maja,' Aimee cried as she ran to her.

The wounded woman held out her hand and gripped Aimee's. Her robes were stained black in the dim light as her own blood seeped up the patterned fabric.

'Get the girl,' Maja whispered in a voice that

gurgled from internal bleeding. 'Don't let them possess the key.'

'I don't understand. What's in the case? What's so important it's worth all this?' Aimee held the dying woman's face as her neck grew limp; Maja's fading strength unable to support the weight of her own head.

'Go to Kayleigh, you don't have a second to lose,' Maja forced the words from her lips. 'She's in danger and so is the world. Do not let the Dark Guard take the key, Aimee. The Stygian must not invoke the Calling. Go now!' demanded Maja with an urgency, laboured through her weakened state, before the last of her strength deserted her.

A gale blew across the entwined, lifeless pair as Forrest stroked Maja's soft, white cheek. She was so young, so beautiful. It was such a waste. A tragic waste.

The soft padding of feet caught Aimee's attention as she lifted her head. At the end of the room she saw a girl run out from the darkness with a panicked expression.

'Kayleigh!' Aimee called out, but the girl did not hear her.

Looking around with wild eyes, as if lost, Kayleigh turned and ran back into the darkness, disappearing as quickly as she came.

Another figure appeared. Her eyes were hidden by sunglasses and her blonde hair tied back into a pony tail. She laughed as she stepped into view.

Aimee recognised the evil, bloodthirsty grin.

It was Cross.

'You want the girl?' Cross called out. 'You want Kayleigh? She's here, with me. In the darkness.'

Walking backwards she retraced her steps, all the time keeping her gaze fixed on Forrest as she melted into the shadows.

Her voice floated through the disused depot.

'Well, Special Constable Forrest. Come get her.'

FOURTEEN

Grappling through the darkness, octopus-like tendrils weakly grasped at Kayleigh. Unable to hold her as she pushed past their slimy grip, they provided enough resistance to slow her down; turning her passage through the gloomy shadows into a struggle.

It was too dark to make out the source of these half-seen tentacles, but to Kayleigh this was a blessing she was thankful for. She'd run into the building and tried to hide in a corner of the long abandoned bus depot, hoping to lose her pursuers in the murky surroundings, but quickly she'd lost her way. The room seemed to grow, the further she walked, and the light had faded until the walls were lost, somewhere in the darkness.

Little could be seen, but Kayleigh felt things moving in the dark, not just those things that touched her skin, but the strange presence of others. She sensed the air was full of feeling, an atmosphere that teemed with anticipation; a desire, waiting to be pulled from the edge of existence and made real.

The sound of crunching underfoot gradually drifted into earshot, getting louder and more defined with every step she took. The darkness lifted, and as it did so she made out a floor scattered with leaves. The autumnal yellows and browns glowed in the evening light that twinkled with a glorious red as the sun began its descent.

Looking around she discovered she was surrounded by tall trees in every direction that cast long, looming shadows in the twilight. The writhing tentacles had retreated but their presence could still be felt, squirming behind the trees as they gently wrapped their slimy appendages around the trunks in a grotesque mockery of ivy.

Cautiously, Kayleigh crept through the wood, her attention caught by flinching shadows and glimmering lights.

A vine shuffled on the tree it grew from, reacting to the passing presence of the confused girl. Twelve green buds opened instantaneously, revealing delicate blooms of fingernail sized beauty. Their purple and blue petals were vibrant in the fading light and as Kayleigh stopped to look on them she realised they were looking back. Within the centre of each flower was a single eye, almost human in design; their pupils moving up and down as they studied their human onlooker.

Strange as this sight was, Kayleigh was not scared. Unsettled as she undoubtedly felt, any feelings of actual fright were vanquished by an unknown sense of familiarity. Her mind, clouded by the surreal surroundings, was unable to recall the source of her feelings.

'Confused?' Cross's voice cut through her thoughts.

Turning round, Kayleigh saw the sadistic smile of her pursuer appear in view as she walked out from behind a tree. Cross smiled at Kayleigh and disappeared again, walking behind the next trunk.

'Do you know where you are?' Cross asked, her question rich with contempt.

Her voice came from behind Kayleigh, making the girl turn and watch the image of the blonde haired killer emerge from behind another tree, far away from the place she'd disappeared from view. In and out of sight she walked, circling and stalking the teenager; appearing from behind seemingly random trees with no earthly logic to the path she was able to take.

'I want that key, Kayleigh,' Cross made every statement sound like a threat. 'I want that pendant.'

'Who are you people?' Kayleigh cried. 'What's going on? Where am I?'

'Oh, don't you recognise this place?' Cross spoke with a patronising tone. 'You were here only last night. How could you forget a land of such disturbing beauty?'

'You murdered my friends!' Kayleigh screamed into the forest.

'They had their time, and they will be forgotten,' Cross's tone changed to one of sincerity. 'Let me help you. I can help you make peace with the world inside. The key in your hand is more than a piece of jewellery. It was no accident you have it, Kayleigh. It felt your pain, your anguish, and it was attracted to them. It is feeding off your dread.'

Kayleigh eyed the object in her hand, but didn't respond to the words of her friend's killer.

'Look to your left,' Cross continued. 'In the clearing. Tell me what you see.'

Looking over her shoulder she caught the sight of a pure white stallion, glowing gold as it reflected the glorious rays of the setting sun. Calmly it swished its tail as it grazed on the grass below its feet. Raising its head into view, Kayleigh saw a singular, large horn, centred between its serene, black eyes that glistened like pearls.

It peacefully shook its mane and continued to feed whilst Kayleigh looked on, dumbfounded.

'This is how it was,' Cross commented, not waiting for a reply. 'This is how it should be.'

Kayleigh's heart began to melt as the sadness subsided.

'Give me the key, Kayleigh,' Cross asked, gently.

'But it doesn't want you,' frustration bubbled behind the young woman's eyes.

Looking back towards the unicorn she marvelled at its beauty, trying to find some reassurance in its vision. This was her protector, her friend. The apparition in her dreams that gave her the strength she carried throughout each day. Last night it had turned on her, its eyes full of hatred, and charged. The beautiful and majestic horn had speared Kayleigh, stabbing her chest and puncturing her lungs.

'When did you wake up, Kayleigh?' Cross asked, as though reading her thoughts. 'Did you feel it pierce your heart? Did you feel yourself die?'

Kayleigh staggered backwards, recognising her words as they echoed Knight's; her colleague they'd held prisoner.

'Did you *ever* wake up?' Cross continued. 'Or have

you pulled us all in? Is this your nightmare?'

Bloodied fingers clawed out from the carpet of dead leaves and gripped the toes of Kayleigh's Converse trainers. Horrified she pulled back and watched as a head rose from the undergrowth. Rotting eyes stared up at her as the creature's neck flapped open, spilling dark, red blood from a ragged wound. Through the blood and dirt that smeared its face, Kayleigh recognised the decomposing features.

'Help us…' came the pathetic rasp of Sam as his broken body crawled through the mud.

In disgust, Kayleigh stepped backwards, tripping on a rock. As she landed on the ground, leaves fell away, revealing the *rock* to be something much more horrific.

'Plea-se… Kay-leigh…' came the disjointed words that filtered through the long grass, emanating from Eleanor's severed head.

'Kay…leigh…' another familiar voice whispered through the wood.

In a panic she got to her feet, looking around for Ollie.

'Kay. . . leigh…' it came again, the sound just behind her left shoulder.

She turned and screamed. On a tree trunk, nailed to the bark, was the remnants of Ollie's face, dismembered like an unmade jigsaw. The wood was stained dark with the dripping blood, whilst the skinned pieces moved as he called out to her. His beard rippled on his chin and his eyes followed the frightened girl as she moved.

Kayleigh ran from the decomposing fragments of her friends, but stumbled on the forest floor as the plants reached out and caught her legs, tripping her.

As she got back to her feet she turned to find the clawing corpse of Sam had disappeared, along with the putrid pieces of Eleanor and Ollie. Their nightmarish presence had vanished from view, but this did little to ease Kayleigh's crumbling mind.

'You want this?' Kayleigh held up the silver object as tears streamed down her face. She pivoted on the spot a few times to allow the hidden Cross to get a good look at the key she held aloft. 'Come get it, you bitch!'

Cross's laugh echoed between the trees as the wind began to scream with the voices of a hundred tormented tongues.

The cacophony was suddenly silenced by the sound of a horse angrily snorting.

The sound gripped Kayleigh's soul and as she looked back to the clearing she found the unicorn was gone.

The sunlight faded as night time took its place.

Red eyes flashed in the darkness.

Kayleigh ran.

Aimee groped her way through the darkness, unnerved at not finding the edge of the room, despite the distance she'd walked.

Surely she must have reached the end of the depot by now?

The Special Constable had chased Cross, but lost her the moment she walked into the dark shadows that clung to the room's edge. Silently she walked on, listening out for both Cross and Kayleigh. The poor girl had looked terrified, but all around was now deathly quiet.

Far away she saw a figure, silhouetted against a far off brightness. Its shoulders shook as it leaned over another figure, sprawled out on the ground.

As her vision struggled to focus Aimee made out the face of a person crying, their tears collecting beneath their eyes.

'Laura,' Aimee called out, but received no response. Greif-stricken, Laura's focus remained intently on the person lying at her feet.

The illumination began to fade, and just before the darkness took them from view, Aimee caught the still face of the motionless body that lay underneath the girl. It was Jake. A trickle of blood dripped down his cheek like a blood-filled tear.

As the corpse and his mourning lover faded into the black, the world around her disappeared once more. All that remained was a faint silver glow, and within this ethereal radiance, shadows of tall trees grew.

Pushing back branches, Kayleigh forced her way through the undergrowth as hooves stamped on the ground from the chasing beast behind her. The unicorn snorted and snarled as it hunted down its prey with a relentless ferocity.

The trees around her seemed to move, clustering together, to prevent her escape. Appearing from the darkness, they closed in and blocked her path, revealing themselves to be vast, writhing tentacles.

Realising she was trapped, Kayleigh turned around to see the demonic eyes of the mythical animal ablaze in the darkness. Like her dream the night before, she had nowhere left to run, nowhere left to hide.

Kayleigh closed her eyes and clasped her pendant as the unicorn lowered its head, its horn now a twisted spike of bone, and galloped forward with a charge.

A thud cracked in her ears, but she felt no pain. Opening her eyes, Kayleigh saw the unicorn knocked on its side, trying to clamber to its feet.

Special Constable Forrest stood in front of her, rubbing her bruised shoulder, and offered a friendly hand.

'Come on, let's go,' the police officer said, locking fingers with the frightened girl and forcing her way past the tree-like tentacles.

The unicorn rose to its feet as, sprinting through the bushes and brambles, the two ran through the darkening wood, searching for an escape.

The beast bellowed an ungodly noise as it trampled through the undergrowth, making short work of the distance between them.

Aimee pushed Kayleigh to the ground, as the horn of the unicorn sliced through the air, grazing Aimee's shoulder. The Special Constable rolled onto her back, but the beast was on top of her, rearing its front hooves and striking her leg.

Aimee screamed in pain as the beast's eyes faded from fiery red to the darkest black.

The animal studied the wounded officer, sniffing her with its blood-soaked nose and relishing the time it took to choose the final deathblow.

Getting to her feet Kayleigh watched in horror as the unicorn toyed with Aimee, slowly goring her side with its gnarled horn.

Kayleigh knew what she had to do. Throughout her

life the unicorn had been a symbol of strength to her, a creature who found her in her dreams and gave her the daily courage to carry on. Since her last dream she'd been terrified the symbol had betrayed her, but it had done no such thing. All the dream had done was to prepare her; to show her at her strongest, her most brave. For the strength didn't come from any symbol, it come from her own core; her own soul.

This was her world. Her nightmare. The key was feeding from her fear. It was time to stop running. To stop giving the key what it wanted and to stop feeling afraid.

She had to give in.

She had to let go.

'You want this?' Kayleigh held up the pendant, the key, Cross desired so badly. 'You want this, you'd better come get it.'

The creature turned to face her, leaving the wounded Special Constable to bleed in the silvery darkness. It snorted with aggression and bared its teeth before stamping its feet and charging toward the seventeen year old.

Kayleigh knew what was coming, and in this dream-fuelled state of déjà vu a calmness took hold. Time seemed to slow as the thud of the animals hooves fell in sync with the booming of her heart. She opened her arms and welcomed the charge towards her. Lowering its head, the unicorn thrust its horn deep into Kayleigh's stomach. A fountain of scarlet liquid gushed from the hole as the beast jerked its head upwards, ripping through her skin and tearing into her left-hand lung. Immediately her breathing shallowed as her lung collapsed, but it only resulted in a gasp of pleasure and a widening of her smile.

Time slowed even further as seconds crawled to minutes. Kayleigh grasped both sides of the steed's vast head and helped guide it up through her body, sinking onto its solid horn. She bit her lip in anticipation, awaiting the final moment and savouring every part of its build-up.

As the horn headed towards her heart she held her breath, and as it sunk deep into her soft, wet insides she let go, both physically and spiritually, screaming with ecstasy.

Another scream echoed through the midnight wood.

But it did not belong to Kayleigh.

As Aimee clambered, unsteadily to her feet she saw Cross, her image shimmering in the silver light like a flickering flame caught in the wind. Her arm dripped with a dark, red liquid than ran from her fingertips and onto the teenager's dead body below.

Cross turned on faltering legs to face the Special Constable and revealed a wound that gushed blood from her face. The key had been thrust into one of her eyes; the decorative spikes sinking into the soft tissue and flesh of the crazed sadist. Kayleigh had planned the attack all along.

The world around them dissolved as the depot began to fade back into view. Cross fell backwards in her disoriented state. Crashing against an appearing window, she fell through the glass, flooding the room with light. The trees faded as strangely as they came and the musty smell of the disused bus depot returned to Aimee's nostrils.

She looked towards Kayleigh who lay at her feet. Blood spilled from a wound and across the young woman's thighs. The end of the unicorn's horn had snapped off her attacker and was still embedded, protruding from her motionless belly.

As the corpse of the spirited teenager stared lifelessly back at her, Aimee noticed a smile on her face, a look of contentment and peace that she had never witnessed all the while she'd known the girl, growing up as her brother's friend.

Thank you, Kayleigh, she thought. *You were very brave.*

Special Constable Forrest walked over to the dying murderer and took Cross by the lapels of her bloodied suit jacket, as she sprawled out, limply over the window frame.

She wrenched the key from her face, revealing the wounded woman's eyes to look like dark craters. So inescapable was the light that fell into them that Aimee couldn't make out exactly what was in their centre. The edges of the two holes appeared to creep from the eye sockets in which they were contained, tainting her face with wisps of darkness that ended in tiny curled tendrils.

Blood bubbled from a deep gash that cut through Cross's neck, a wound inflicted from the fall, when a piece of broken glass had sliced across her throat.

'You fucking bitch,' Aimee cursed, as she watched the bubbling fade.

Letting go of her suit, Aimee let Cross's head fall backwards, slumping over the window frame and opening the gory wound further with a spray of arterial blood.

The crimson spray soaked the volunteer officer and startled her. Awaking Cross, her vice-like grip took hold of Aimee's wrist and shocked the Special Constable into opening her hand. The key fell from her fingers and was snatched away.

Weakened as she was, but with jittery movements, Cross crawled out the window.

Making her escape, she didn't rise to her feet but crawled on the floor. Her body bent backwards whilst her hands and feet scuttled over the ground in a crab-like manner, but with the grace and elegance of a slithering snake. Her tongue took on a new shape as it lashed the air.

Aimee tried to grab the unnatural abomination, but she moved too quickly and scampered away. Climbing through the window herself and back outside, Forrest watched as Cross scaled a building, clambering up an exterior wall with the ease of a galloping spider. She gave chase on the ground, but by the time she'd got to the other side of the dilapidated construction the freakish female had made her descent, down the far wall and, with the key in her hand, was almost at her destination.

That destination was Scullin.

FIFTEEN

Outnumbered, but still in control, the hulkish leader stood at the edge of a man-made chasm. The deep hole was dug a few years ago, at the beginning of a construction contract that crumbled in the height of the recession. It was to be the foundation of a great, high-rise office block, and a chance to revitalise the area. But as the financial backing fell through, the construction team had moved out, leaving behind a huge crater. Over time its bottom had been filled with rubble, rubbish and materials that were left around the site; thrown into it by bored kids looking for something to do.

The broken glass, jagged brickwork and twisted iron stuck up like spikes from a jungle trap, making the pit a deadly drop.

Laura's feet dangled over the edge, held in this precarious position by Scullin. One of his large hands gripped both her wrists as she froze within his clutches.

At his feet lay Jake's body, collapsed face first into the dirt. The ground surrounding his head had stained a brownish red from the blood that escaped an unseen wound.

The crawling Cross reached her leader and passed him the key. A smile faintly appeared on his face as he took the silver object with his free remaining hand.

'You have done well,' he thanked the twisted form that presented him his prize.

Cross replied by flicking her sharp, arrow-like tongue in the air.

Scullin turned his attention back to the girl at his mercy, and as he did so a wooden pole was driven through the black pit of one of Cross's eyes; her deathblow delivered behind his back. Her body began to constrict as an ear shredding howl escaped from her gaping mouth. Her one remaining eye looked up to see Taal, holding his staff and twisting it further into her brain. His face was cut and bloodied, his lip swollen and his left eye half closed, but with a determined look he continued to force his staff into the creature before him.

Cross's back arched to the point of breaking as her arms and legs buckled under her own weight. As her screams faded her body cracked and snapped, rolling in on itself and leaving a collection of distorted limbs protruding at vomit inducing angles.

Scullin turned to face Taal.

'Coming back for more, little man?' he taunted. 'It's over. I have both keys.'

'This fight's far from done. The keys are useless without the case,' Taal raised his staff, ready to attack. 'Put the girl down.'

'Gladly,' came Scullin's swift reply as he dropped her to the ground.

Laura tried to right herself as her feet touched down but she stumbled, falling backwards into the pit. Scullin didn't even wait for her screams to end before he swung his first punch. Taal nimbly dodged the careering fist. He was unlucky to have been caught by Scullin's blows before, allowing the boy and girl to distract him; his thoughts concerned with their safety. This was a mistake. There were greater things at stake than the lives of two budding adults.

He dodged another fist and jabbed his staff, the end striking Scullin in the neck, making his adversary stumble with pain.

Now there were no distractions, Taal was focused. The contents of that case had to be held by the Servitude, the Calling had to be prevented.

Aimee watched the duelling pair as she ran to the aid of her unconscious brother. Kneeling beside him, she lifted his head and smiled as his eyelids began to open. She picked up his glasses that lay beside him and placed them on his nose. One lens was shattered and the other filthy with dirt, but he looked at her through them and returned her smile.

'I thought you were dead!' Her face softened as she stroked his hair.

'Where's Laura?' Jake asked, concerned as his memories returned.

Aimee answered her brother with a sorrowful expression. 'I'm sorry, Jake,' his sister replied, 'Laur-'

Her sentence was cut short by a shrill cry for help. The pair scrambled to the edge of the deep hole and looked over the side. Their hearts jumped, a mixture of relief and alarm as quarter of the way down they saw his girlfriend. Her dress had caught on an iron rod that stuck out from the side of the pit, and against all odds the fabric was supporting her, leaving her dangling over the broken glass and jagged bricks that lay at the bottom.

'Help me!' She looked towards Jake and Aimee, pleading for rescue.

Scullin dropped to his knees, hobbled by the carefully placed strike into his heel. Even knelt down he was taller than his opponent. He held his tongue, stifling an expression of pain.

'Give in or face your death,' Taal threatened.

'One of us has to die today,' Scullin replied, getting back to his feet. 'You know that as much as I.'

'So be it,' Taal answered, spinning with balletic poise and swinging his staff towards the large man's head.

Holding his arm up to protect himself, Scullin's powerful forearm took the impact. It knocked him sideways, lifting him from the ground and sending him crashing into the wall of one of the buildings. His large bulk smashed a hole through the crumbling brickwork.

Taal observed as the fallen man dusted himself off and slowly tried to get to his feet. Holding his arms out and constructing a premeditated shape with his fingers, the Servant of the Sacred Whisper began to quietly chant a sentence of secret words, long protected by the practitioners of the Servitude.

Sweat drenched his skin and his muscles shook with an unknown exertion, but as he continued to chant, cracks grew in the walls and snaked up the masonry, spreading their destructive lines until, with a mighty crash, the building caved in, burying Scullin in an avalanche of bricks and mortar.

A thick black liquid seeped out from the fallen debris, and after watching it for a moment, Taal turned his back on the pile of rubble and made his way to the briefcase. With his enemy vanquished he did not care for keys. The Calling would be prevented and the Servitude had all the time in the world to work out how to open the case and retrieve its revered contents. Patience was a valuable power.

He'd only taken a few steps when he heard the sound of falling stone. By the time he'd turned round Scullin had clawed his way free from his temporary tomb.

Deep, black cavities looked out from Scullin's face, exposed now his sunglasses had been crushed, and buried their vacant, horrific gaze into the lone survivor of the travelling cult members.

Reasoning with him was an impossible task, and before Aimee could suggest the best plan to help, Jake was already on his way, climbing down the deep hole that his girlfriend was hanging over; only held from falling by the strength of her denim dress.

'I'm coming, baby,' he called out, reassuring her as he picked out his pathway on the tricky descent.

Scullin charged at Taal. A sidestep saw the robed figure avoid the attack, but the assault was not over. Fists rained down in anger on the man from India, and with all the skill his training had developed over the years he dodged, weaved, blocked and countered to protect himself from the onslaught.

Jake gripped onto the rock as he leant closer, his fingertips just out of reach of the blue material that was hooked onto the end of a snapped support rod.

'Please Jake,' Laura looked into the eyes of her boyfriend and cried. 'I don't want to die.'

Straining to extend his reach he tried to ignore the sound of fabric slowly tearing.

The faintest of glimpse in Scullin's cavernous eyes was all it took for Taal to give his adversary the edge in battle. Momentarily breaking his concentration, he found his staff wrenched from his hands as he mistimed his next attack. Pushed to the ground with a swift kick, the Servant of the Sacred Whisper could only watch as Scullin snapped his staff in two and tossed it aside.

Defenceless, he held his hands above him, trying to recount the call that would aid him now. The sight of those eyes had thrown him, planting a seed of fear into his mind. As he wrestled the growing weed from his thoughts, his much needed incantations eluded his consciousness.

The rock in Jake's hand gave way, crumbling under the strain. He fell forward and dug his fingers into the side wall. Finding a secure handle, he stopped his fall and reached out, grasping hold of Laura's dress. Carefully he unhooked it from the metal rod and pulled it towards him, the sound of denim ripping, growing louder.

Aimee watched as Scullin towered over Taal and picked him up, clean off the ground, holding him at eye level. Below, her brother was clinging to the rock face with his fingertips in an attempt to save his girlfriend.

They both needed her help.

'Not so formidable without your weapon,' Scullin mocked in the face of his beaten opponent.

'You underestimate our resourcefulness,' Taal spoke with his usual calm, the fear in his face had faded. 'And our ability to play dirty.'

With the speed of a striking praying mantis, Taal jabbed at one of Scullin's eyes, burying his fingers knuckle deep into the hole.

The monk-like man was thrown to the ground as Scullin collapsed with agony, holding his face.

'It's time to put an end to this,' Taal exclaimed as he stood over his wounded combatant.

A girl's scream cut through the air.

Taal turned, distracted by the noise. Scullin thrust his hand forward, gripping Taal's throat and squeezed.

Black dripped from his wounded eye and poured down his face. He spat the strange liquid as he spoke with a grin.

'Yes. Yes it is.'

The strain on the dress had proven too much and tore away in Jake's hands. Laura screamed as she felt herself fall.

Running to their aid, Aimee looked over the edge to see Jake grasping hold of his girlfriend's arm. Her brother had leant forward in desperation and caught his lover, whilst at the same time finding another secure handhold with which to steady them both. Stretched and strained to his absolute limit, Jake was unable to turn, let alone find a way back up.

'Hang on Jake, I'm coming,' Aimee called out.

Taal would have to wait, Aimee thought as she climbed towards them.

Reaching out she took hold of her brother's hand.

'Thank you sis,' he said as their fingers entwined.

'We aren't out of this yet,' she warned. 'Keep hold of Laura. Laura, when I pull, you kick your feet against the rock. Try and walk yourself up. Jake, you pull and do the same, okay?'

The pair listened to her instructions and slowly they began to drag themselves out of the hole.

Laura clambered to the top, scratched and filthy but smiling to be safe in her boyfriend's arms.

A frail voice called out, making Aimee turn. Taal lay on the ground, his eyes milky white and bleeding.

'Special Constable Forrest,' he called out, weakly.

Panicked for the whereabouts of Scullin she scanned the landscape. Although badly wounded and leaving a trail of thick, almost black blood in his wake, she saw him staggering across the construction site, towards the briefcase.

'Don't you think you're getting away from me, you fucker,' she spat as she got to her feet and sprinted towards him. 'Jake,' she called back to her brother. 'Get yourself and Laura up to the squad car and stay there. There's a radio in the front. Call for back up. If it doesn't work the first time, keep trying.'

Briefcases, keys, neither of these mattered to the Special Constable. What mattered to her was this man had been responsible for the deaths of many good people, and he was not getting away with it.

'Not so fast, asshole,' she shouted as she approached him, standing between him and the case. 'You've got a lot to answer for. You're under arrest.'

'Ha ha ha,' Scullin laughed her off. His voice burbled as he bled, but his injuries looked less than before, as if his wounds were already healing. He looked stronger, threatening once again. 'Your laws do not concern me,' his voice boomed.

'Stay away from-' Taal's voice was too weak to carry over the thunder claps that erupted in the sky.

Rain began to fall in torrents as the storm finally broke, soaking them all within seconds. Aimee lunged forward, kicking Scullin in the place guaranteed to make any man drop. He was no exception. Gasping in pain, he fell to his knees.

Holding her hand flat she drove the base of her palm into the side of his neck. His skin felt like granite as she made contact, but despite the pain that shot up her arm, she was relieved to see him wince.

The ground around them was quickly sodden, turning the dusty landscape into a muddy bog. Its sudden slippery surface took Forrest by surprise, and as she blocked a swing by Scullin she lost her grip underfoot and fell.

Taking the advantage he rose to his feet and punched her in the stomach, then to the face. Aimee tried to stand, but another blow to the cheek sent her crashing back down. The pain surged through her body and her head span. She crawled around in the mud trying to find her balance and evade Scullin's powerful assault, but a kick to the thigh stopped her escape and sent her writhing in agony.

Dragging her free from the mire, Scullin lifted her above his head.

'You have bothered me for the last time,' he growled.

Walking towards the briefcase he held the Special Constable aloft, crushing her between his hands. She screamed as she felt her left leg snap, the bone being unable to withstand the pressure exerted on it by the abnormally strong Scullin.

With each step he took closer to his goal he squeezed that much harder. Aimee screamed again as her right arm gave way, snapping at the forearm in his terrible grip.

She tried to fight, but the pain was too much, her stubborn resolve had, at last been destroyed. Scullin had beaten her.

Special Constable Aimee Forrest looked to the heavens and wondered if it was all true. When death laid its claim on her would she discover an afterlife? Would she meet with PC Osborne again? She prayed she would.

As he approached the briefcase, the material from Scullin's jacket began to unthread. Holes ripped in the fragmenting fabric, revealing cuts that etched across his skin. He clenched his jaw as he watched the wounds appear, slicing into his arms and chest from some unseen force.

The Eolhx was at work once again.

Bearing the pain, he stopped for a moment and

flexed his muscles, allowing the blood to pump faster from the growing gashes.

He threw Aimee to the ground and she screamed in agony as her flesh met with the same fate. Skin peeled from her body as she tried to crawl away from the enchanted circle. She slipped in the mud and fell face first, but clawed at the boggy earth, finding purchase and slowly pulled herself free. Feeling the assault abate as she reached safe ground, she turned to view her enemy.

A half smile spread across Scullin's face as he watched his lacerations slowly begin to disappear.

'Your tricks don't work on me, old man,' he called out to Taal. 'You are weak and dying. Your incantations have lost their strength. They are fading.' He laughed as a bloody slash opened across his cheek, only to seal back up again. 'These pitiful attacks are no match to the speed with which I heal.'

The brutish figure bent down and took hold of the briefcase.

'The Calling shall succeed,' he roared into the storm. 'The great ones matter little where the ceremony takes place. Here is as good as any. I even have my sacrifice,' he glanced towards Aimee. 'We shall welcome our first masters, and then you will understand what it truly means to fear the dark!'

Taking the key from his hand he placed it into one of the ornate locks. The small spikes that covered its surface filled the grooves and held snugly into position. With a sense of victory he loosened his collar and pulled out a small chain that easily snapped, freeing the second key from its hiding place. Holding the case at eye level he aimed the silvery charm towards the lock, lining its raised edges to the correlating, decorative pits.

The apocalypse was mere moments away and all Aimee could do was watch; an enforced witness in her own broken body.

Scullin let out a scream.

But it wasn't the sound of triumph.

As he dropped both the key and case, the cry was that of blood curdling agony. A red patch of liquid seeped through his shirt before his chest erupted as something exploded through his ribcage; driven through from the other side.

He stumbled forwards, onto his knees, pawing at his own bleeding body and crumpling with pain. As he fell to the ground he revealed a young woman stood behind him. Her hand dripped with his life juices and in her clenched palm was a pointed, jagged object.

The weapon's gnarled, boney structure was familiar to Aimee's eyes, as was the girl's face, but it took a moment for both to register.

It was the unicorn's horn.

And it was Kayleigh!

The girl smiled at Aimee before she took the horn in both hands, reaching above her head then driving it down, hard into Scullin's neck. It parted his flesh with unnatural ease as Kayleigh buried her weapon along his spine and deep into his skull. His lifeless shell slumped further forward, collapsing onto the ground with a large thud.

There would be no healing from these wounds. Not with an object from his own dark realm.

'They never teach you to check for a pulse at cop school,' Kayleigh quipped with a wry smile.

'Kayleigh!' Aimee shouted with joy as the pair met in an embrace.

'Careful.' Kayleigh winced as she pulled herself free from the smothering hug. 'I'm still a bit tender.'

Taal lay on his back, struggling for air, listening to the chatter of the two heroic women. An uncharacteristic smile spread across his face as he drew his final breath, his sightless eyes staring at the dawning of a starless night.

SIXTEEN

Disobeying his sister's command, Jake ran to the centre of the construction site, tired of waiting at the wreck of the police car and worried about Aimee. She always could take care of herself, but this was different, Scullin was no ordinary *idiot on a Saturday night.*

For the first time in her life, Aimee was pleased he hadn't listened. His worried, but warm smile greeted her as he ran toward the Special Constable and Kayleigh.

They hugged, and as Aimee's chin rested on his shoulder she noticed something, half trodden into the mud. Digging it from the earth, she discovered it was a car key; the Audi logo giving her a clear indication of which car it belonged to.

As Kayleigh and Jake headed back to the police car, Aimee staggered across the construction site.

'I've just got to check something out. You guys head back up to Laura and get help. I'll be fine,' she reassured their worried expressions.

By the time the teenagers reached their destination Laura had good news; she'd managed to reach someone on the radio. Despite the immense damage done to the car, the radio was working perfectly. Police and ambulances were being dispatched and would be with them soon.

Jake set the briefcase down, using it as a stool whilst he studied the two, strange shaped keys he'd salvaged from the site of the massacre.

Thunder gently echoed from far away, blown from the city skies by the powerful winds.

'Don't be fooled,' Kayleigh said as she eased herself onto a seat of the smashed police car. 'That storm may be heading off but the rain will be here for days.'

She sat, hypnotised for a while, as she watched the rain drops lightly splatter the windscreen in front of her. The sound of them hitting the roof gave her a pleasing sense of security.

Breaking free of her trance, Kayleigh turned to Laura as they sat together.

'You okay?' she asked.

The Audi stood, untouched, next to the blood soaked limousine that had acted as a prison to her and a crypt to her colleague.

'Osborne,' Aimee muttered remorsefully as she walked by, stopping for a moment to gaze once more on his face; peacefully blank in its eternal slumber.

She allowed a minute of silence as a mark of respect before leaving her moment of mourning. Forrest stood by the black Audi and took another look through the tinted windows. She could have sworn she'd seen movement from the other side of the glass earlier today.

Everything had happened so fast she hadn't time to check properly. But now she could.

The Special Constable pressed the unlock button. Yellow sidelights flashed and a whirring mechanism indicated the doors had unlocked. Aimee cautiously gripped the door handle and clicked it open. Gently she pulled it free, but as she got halfway the door was suddenly pushed wide by a heavy force. Something large fell from the backseat, thudding onto the ground.

'It unnerves me how you do that,' a voice rasped down the phone. 'I received word you were dead.'

'Consider me the proverbial cat,' the blonde haired woman replied, with a chilling calmness. She placed her sunglasses back onto the bridge of her nose.

'Remind me to never underestimate you, Cross,' came the retort. 'Do you have the prize?' The phone crackled, struggling to hold its connection.

'Not yet,' Cross reclined into the soft leather of a luxury swivel chair, whilst a sigh emanated from the speaker. She heard the rain gently tap against the window of her office, overlooking the city. The storm was returning. 'But there's still time… Yes,' her patience sounded strained as she replied to a question, muffled by the weakening signal, 'we have an agent in the field. Sheppard is in position.'

'It works!' Jake shouted in amazement, startling the two women.

Laura and Kayleigh both looked to see the keys inserted into the briefcase, the spiky points fitting perfectly into the slits and grooves of the decorative locks.

'Jake, you stupid idiot, that's evidence. Aimee will kill you!' Kayleigh warned him, but he was in no mood to listen. Curiosity had taken hold.

He flicked the catches and the locks sprang open.

As Jake gripped the case the wind began to howl with an increasing ferocity.

Cautiously he raised the lid, but was shocked by the sudden spring action that took hold. It burst open, falling from his lap as he jumped in surprise.

The case fell on its side. Jake and Laura scrabbled to rescue its contents, but were too late. A large, solitary envelope, fell to the floor. Laura's hands reached to grab it, but the wind took hold of the curled corners and carried it across the construction site.

Aimee gasped as she looked down by her feet at the foul surprise that was wrapped in a familiar denim dress. A head of long, brown hair half covered a sunken face; shrivelled and lifelessly grey in colour. Their eyes were a muted blue, locked in an expression of terror and devoid of the spark of life.

'Laura,' Aimee whispered, her brain racing to understand what she was seeing.

Looking further up the site she could make out the three figures of Jake, Kayleigh and *Laura.*

Her mind cast back to the shooting outside the bank. The numbers of people in suits and sunglasses. There *had* been another woman in their group.

But how…?

The words of Maja drifted through her mind, *Each of the Dark Guard has a unique way in which their powers manifest…*

In the distance the Special Constable saw the girl in the denim dress stood behind the others as they crowded round the empty briefcase. Aimee ran towards them as the girl raised her hands above her head, clutching something long and pointed whilst stepping closer to Kayleigh and Jake.

As the gales grew stronger the envelope lifted, high into the air. Over the fence and across the city it sailed, past the fountains and through the centre until it fell with grace, landing in a dark, grimy alleyway. As the sodden package drifted downwards it dislodged a pile of rubbish, knocking used condoms, empty cigarette packets, even a battered old memory stick into an ephemeral river, created by the blocked drains.

The envelope itself was next to be caught by the current and followed the stream of filthy flood water until, exposed to the prevailing winds once more, it took flight. Soaring into the air, it danced one last time with the rain before it pirouetted earthwards and fell through the crack of an open window.

The resident of the flat had slumbered all afternoon in front of the television, and was rudely awoken by the soggy envelope, slopping its wet mass, squarely in their face.

Startled at first by the damp encounter, the woman sat up and rubbed herself dry. Intrigued, she made her way to the kitchen table, placed her glasses on the end of her nose and opened the sealed flap.

Her muscles contracted as her body stiffened, shocked by the sight before her. She stumbled backwards and fell against a worktop, holding her hands out to try and steady herself. Something slithered just out of the corner of her vision as growing circles danced in front of her eyes, shimmering with an oil-like vibrancy as they swirled through the air in wild rotations. The walls of her flat crawled towards the ceiling, allowing off-green vines to force their way into her abode like a swarm of inquisitive tentacles.

She held her stomach as she felt it protest, gurgling from the enforced nausea. The circles in her vision span faster and faster until suddenly they collided together, exploding like static from an old television.

Euphoria gripped her heart, saturated with an intense awakening of abject terror. Her eyes remained wide open, unable to even blink at the sights before her.

It was as if all of creation had stopped still, frozen in microcosm before her eyes; a picture postcard of eternity that hung from invisible hooks in all its terrifying beauty.

Thunder cracked loudly in the sky as she held her hand to her mouth, almost obscuring the words of her native language as she exclaimed in disbelief, 'O Boże!'

Every tale must have a beginning.

This is where we will start.

ABOUT THE AUTHOR

J. R. Park is an author of horror fiction and co-founder of the Sinister Horror Company. His books have received critical praise; enough to encourage further scribblings on the dark and macabre.

He resides in Bristol, UK. An avid music fan, he can often be found watching live music in various venues across the city. If you see him nodding in approval to a wave of white noise with a faraway look in his eye, then chances are another book is on the cards.

The following preview contains the introduction and first chapter to J. R. Park's next novella.

MAD DOG

J.R Park

Introduction

Darkdale prison was subject to a second serious incident in as many months. In order to understand the events that took place a series of interviews were conducted. What follows is the compiled testimonies of witnesses to this second atrocity.

Chapter 1

Hannah Miller (University Student): You know I wasn't there, right? I had no intention of visiting, even before that bastard Mooney got sent down. Sure, you could say I *met* Mooney. *Encountered him*, would be more appropriate. *Mad Dog*, they called him, right? Jimmy used to say that in his letters.

Have you ever seen him? In the flesh I mean. Everyone saw the mugshot in the newspapers. Ugly son of a bitch wasn't he? That scar running down his forehead and over his eye socket. His right eye all cloudy, grey and fucked up. God knows why he didn't get an eye patch, or get it removed and replaced with a glass one. That's what I did. You might think he looked scary in those photos, but that's nothing compared to seeing the man for real. They say there's a monster inside all of us. With Mooney, that monster was well and truly out.

I guess that's why you're talking to me. Want to know what it was like to meet the legend before he was taken to Darkdale? A bit of background for your story.

I hadn't been at University very long, still in

Fresher's fortnight. Two weeks of drinking may be hard on the liver but I didn't feel it. I don't really get hangovers and all that going out had gotten me relaxed to my new surroundings very quickly.

The fortnight was coming to a close and we were all going on another fancy dress pub crawl. You wouldn't believe the amount of money I spent on costumes. This time round it was characters from kid's books and TV shows and I went for the classic Little Red Riding Hood, thought it would be fun. Red hooded shawl, shocking red nails, lipstick to match, short skirt, stockings. You know the look. Even bought a basket that I carried round with the mask of a wolf in it. I filled the mask with newspaper to give it bulk. Make it look like I cut the monster's head off. After a few pubs the basket and mask disappeared. No idea where I left them. But better to lose them than my purse. I've done that a few times now.

So the night is going well. Ally and Rach are on it, and I'm matching them drink for drink, shot for shot. The boys came sniffing round as usual, peacocking with all that alpha male bullshit, but we weren't interested. We were on a mission to reach oblivion and then dance our asses off until the sun came up. Fuck those Rugby boys. They make my skin crawl with their own self-importance. Never impressed me and never will.

Sorry. I'm getting side tracked.

So the basket's long gone and the drinks are flying down our throats. As I order a round of Jager bombs I'm told the card machine has stopped working. Fine time for that to happen. And although I still have my purse on me, there's no money in it. Stumbling out of the Huntsman I head to the nearest cashpoint. Surprise, surprise the thing's empty. Everyone else has already done what I've done and beat me to it. So I mash the keypad in frustration and head down the street looking for the next one.

Now, I know I said I was comfortable with my new surroundings, but that didn't mean I knew them all too well; especially with a bloodstream rapidly filling with alcohol. I really couldn't tell you how I ended up where I did, clearly I took a wrong turning somewhere, but before I know it I'm in a deserted side street, wandering down an alley with my hand on the wall to keep myself upright. The silence is making my ears ring and the streetlights have all disappeared. Thunder rumbles somewhere off in the distance, just like in some crappy horror movie, and I start looking around, trying to get my bearings. I never knew it could get so dark in a city.

Suddenly my mind sharpens. I realise my situation. I'm lost and I'm alone. Pulling out my phone from my bag I go to call Rach when the sound of something awful echoes down the alley.

If I sounded a little blasé when I started this story, that's because I've told it so many times. After a while it becomes nothing but words. I've tried my best to divorce all feeling from them. But let me tell you, right here, right now, whatever that sound was scared the living shit out of me.

I jumped and my heart beat so hard I thought I was going to keel over. I watched the light of my phone as it fell to the floor and skated across the ground. It stopped abruptly as it careered into something big and solid. The bluish glow was faint but effective enough, and slowly my eyes made sense of the shapes it was illuminating.

At first I saw the outline of a face. The contours of a cheek and nose nearly touching the ground. It was small, child-like. A little girl, crawling in the dark. Long hair splayed out from two pigtails on her head. Her blonde bunches were filthy; muddied from soaking up what I thought was dirty puddle water. I couldn't have been more wrong.

She hadn't seen me. Probably blinded by the light of my phone.

I watched as she stretched out her hands, gripped the ground and pulled herself along, dragging her belly over the concrete. She was shivering and I went to call out; to ask if she was alright, but that noise came again and took my voice. A dog-like growl.

Like a frightened deer, my instincts told me to freeze.

A patter of footsteps, like bare feet running across concrete, caught my ears.

The girl rolled onto her back. The light of my phone fully illuminated her face, and I can see these awful slashes across her cheeks, drenching her in blood. Flaps of torn skin dangle from her face. It was just horrible. Her eyes were like saucers, wide with terror, as she stared back into the black.

Another growl echoed round the alley, only this time much louder.

Much closer.

The girl went to scream, but she fainted before she could make a sound, her head hitting the concrete with a sickening thud. A dark puddle of what must have been blood oozed from her cracked skull and I watched, stunned, as her body gently rocked from the influence of something else. Someone hidden in the dark.

Holding my breath, I tried to focus on the darkness. I tried to peer through the night and eventually my perseverance paid off. Slowly I made out a large figure, squatted and hunched over the poor, unconscious girl. At first I thought he was wearing a fur coat, but as I saw his huge muscles flex underneath, I realised it wasn't a coat at all. He was completely naked.

This was how I met Mitch *Mad Dog* Mooney.

I didn't know it was him of course, back then he wasn't the notorious figure he is now.

His hands were huge, ending in points, like claws that gripped hold of the poor girl. His ears seemed to rise above his hair, and his eyes; his eyes glowed in the dark, reflecting the light from my phone like a cat caught in headlights.

But it's when I traced the sounds of grunts and tearing, when I saw his mouth, that I felt my legs nearly collapse from under me. Maybe it was a mixture of the shadows and alcohol, but his jaw looked like it was pulled out of shape, into a weird, elongated snout. I know, crazy right? But the first thing I thought of when I saw him was the mask I'd stuffed with newspaper and lost with my basket.

He opened his mouth and exposed a set of over-sized teeth. I winced as I watched him sink them into the flesh of that little girl. Her ribs snapped as he bit down, and as he tore apart her chest, I watched those broken ribs drop to the floor. I wanted to run, my brain screamed at me to get out of there, but like a bad bout of sleep paralysis, my body refused to listen. He took another bite, this time into the soft flesh of her stomach. My own belly stirred in disgust, but I couldn't take my eyes off the trails of gristle and skin that hung from his chin, dripping in blood.

It was only when he stopped chewing those monstrous jaws and his eyes looked up into mine did the spell slowly begin to subside. Those eyes glowed with a bright intensity, and even then I noticed the difference in his right eye. It was a subtle shade darker.

My foot edged back slowly away from him, but I kept him squarely in my vision. He rose from his crouching position and I watched him tower above me.

And then the little girl turned her head.

She looked at me, her face all twisted and weak like my Grandmother's before she died. Tears glistened in her eyes and her own blood poured from her mouth as she wrestled with her words. It was low and very faint, like a whisper. But I heard it clear enough. A warning from someone that had already accepted their death.

'Go away!'

I wasn't about to argue. I had no choice. My cover had been blown. I was no longer the scared deer, I was the hunted rabbit. I turned and ran, but he was on me too quickly. I felt him catch hold of my cape and pull me backwards. Stupid costume! I landed on my ass but rolled away, instinct and adrenaline propelling me forward. Climbing back to my feet I tried to sprint off, but was swiped in the side by one of those awful claws. A pain shot up my body as I fell forward, crashing into a wheelie bin. It knocked the wind from me as I slumped to my knees, dazed and clutching at my side.

I didn't look up to see him stood over me; *I could sense it.*

I could feel the warmth of his hunger, the evil in those eyes.

The sound of his panting grew louder as he bent down to look at me. The fucker knew he had me trapped. His breath was warm against my skin, but I refused to look. I couldn't accept this nightmare. I wouldn't allow it in.

I swear I could almost feel his teeth on my skin.

And then I lashed out. With my clutch bag still in

my hand I swung at his head, hoping maybe I'll get a shot at that dodgy eye. Not a hope in hell! It was like lighting the touch paper. All of a sudden he launched at me. I looked up to see those glowing eyes, the snapping of those terrible teeth; the ripping claws that reached out for me.

I turned and clung to the wall, trying to pull myself up and get away, but he knocked me to the floor and was on top of me with a strength I couldn't fight.

Everything went red as he snapped and clawed. I held my hands up, pushing at his face to fend him off, but he just kept coming. Blood poured down my fingers, making them indistinguishable from the nail-varnished tips I'd so lovingly painted hours earlier. Had he biten them off? I couldn't tell. Obvious now, huh?

The pain going through my body was so immense, so overwhelming, that I just stopped feeling it. Every strike to my face, every bite towards my head left a washed out stinging sensation, muted with shock.

I'm not sure if I remember the next bit, or my brain filled in the blanks with its own story, as when I recall it, it's like I'm watching it from afar. Like I'm watching it on a movie.

My arms won't move, I'm exhausted and blood is pouring down me. He grabs my throat and picks me up; lifts me so we're at eye-level, my feet dangling uselessly in mid-air. I'm done fighting and I watch as he pulls his other arm back like he's ready to swing at me; tear my face off with that huge claw. His lips curl up like an angry dog, exposing his teeth that are now dripping in *my* blood.

This is it then, Little Red Riding Hood, I remember thinking to myself as I finally give in.

I close my eyes tight. The stinging and injuries

make my face feel strange.

Like a mask.

The next thing I know I hear a voice.

'Over there!' a man called out. 'Put the girl down.'

All of a sudden there's a strange sound and I'm gritting my teeth as my whole body tightens and a new type of pain courses through me. I feel Mooney let go and I fall to the floor; the pain dissipating as quickly as it came.

I roll over and understand what's happened. I watch as more tasers are fired at him. The electrodes dig into his body. He struggles with them for a moment, trying to pull them from his skin as he staggers towards the police, but eventually he drops. I'm trying to stay awake, elated I'm alive, but the shock is all too much for me. As I fight unconsciousness I look over to the fallen Mooney. The monster does indeed look bestial, but as I begin to accept my safety he appears more human.

They say fear makes the wolf grow bigger. Well security makes the monster more tragic.

My sympathies reach out to my attacker and I can't stop smiling as I look at the unconscious man next to me. I hear the police kneel by my side, but their words are a blur. I look at Mooney's scarred and beaten face and I see a pained peace in his slow breaths.

Tears rolls down my cheeks, only they're not tears. I understand this when I go to brush them away. As I wipe my eye I feel something long and thin poking into it. But it's not going *in*, it's coming *out*. My fingers feel around the edge of the eye socket, itself nothing more than the rim to a hole in my face. I follow the fleshy cord that hangs out of my skull, scooping up the organic twine in my hand until I come to a dead, fleshy orb at the end. *My eye.*

Sympathy turns to anger, but *his* expression remains the same.

As I looked on, I hoped he'd die that night.

A part of me thinks he did too.

TERROR BYTE – J. R. PARK

Street tough Detective Norton is a broken man.

Still grieving the murder of his girlfriend he is called to investigate the daylight slaughter of an entire office amid rumours of a mysterious and lethal computer program. As the conspiracy unfolds the technological killer has a new target.
Fighting for survival Norton must also battle his inner demons, the wrath of MI5 and a beautiful but deadly mercenary only known as Orchid.

Unseen, undetectable and unstoppable.
In the age of technology the most deadly weapon is a few lines of code.

TERROR BYTE

J.R. PARK

"Truly a horror tale for the modern digital age." - Duncan P Bradshaw, author of Class Three

"Fast paced, action-packed, intricately plotted and filled with technological paranoia." - Duncan Ralston, author of Gristle & Bone

"He manages to combine gore, sex, humour and suspense with a gripping story line."- Love Horror Books

"J. R. Park's new novella Terror Byte could be the story to bring horror back to technology based adventures." - UK Horror Scene

"Jesus. What the fuck is this?" - Vincent Hunt, creator of The Red Mask From Mars

PUNCH – J. R. PARK

It's carnival night in the seaside town of Stanswick Sands and tonight blood will stain the beach red.
Punch and Judy man, Martin Powell, returns after ten years with a dark secret. As his past is revealed Martin must face the anger of the hostile townsfolk, pushing him to the very edge of sanity.
Humiliated and stripped of everything he holds dear, Martin embarks on a campaign of murderous revenge, seeking to settle scores both old and new.

The police force of this once sleepy town can't react quick enough as they watch the body count grow at the hands of a costumed killer.
Can they do enough to halt the malicious mayhem of the twisted Punch?

PUNCH

J. R. Park

"Fast-paced, uncompromising, and doesn't pull any punches whatsoever." – DLS Reviews

"It's a heartbreaking tale. I'd strongly urge anyone, looking for a straight forward raw read to buy this as soon as possible."- HorrorWorlds.com

"Sharp writing, solid characterization and with one of the most memorable endings in recent memory." – Ginger Nuts of Horror

"Graphical nightmares effectively place the reader in an uneasy position." - Horror Palace

"A rousing combo of parental angst and seething evil. A great spin on the post-modern serial killer." - Daniel Marc Chant, author of Mr Robespierre

"A hard hitting story of the darker side of life in a sleepy little seaside town." - Paul Pritchard, Amazon reviewer

UPON WAKING – J. R. PARK

What woke you from your sleep?
Was it the light coming through the curtains? The traffic from the street outside?

Or was it the scratching through the walls? The cries of tormented anguish from behind locked doors? The desperate clawing at the woodwork from a soul hell bent on escape?

Welcome to a place where the lucky ones die quickly.

Upon waking, the nightmare truly begins.

UPON WAKING – J. R. PARK

UPON WAKING J.R. PARK

"Upon Waking is a novel that will challenge you as a reader." – Ginger Nuts of Horror

"An absolute masterclass in gut-wrenchingly violent horror." – DLS Reviews

"J. R. Park has written one of the most painfully twisted books I have ever had the pleasure of reading. I loved it!" – " Book Lovers

"Justin Park needs help. I can't think of any other way of putting it. The part of his mind that this story came from must be one of the darkest places in the universe. His writing however, is just wonderful." – Confessions of a Reviewer

"It's almost like poetry in form and prose. But it's a trick. A fantastically disgusting trick." – Thomas S Flowers, author of Reinhiet

"Seriously – buy this book!" – Matt Shaw, author of Sick B*stards.

For up to date information on the work of J. R. Park visit:

JRPark.co.uk
Facebook.com/JRParkAuthor
Twitter @Mr_JRPark

For further information on the Sinister Horror Company visit:

SinisterHorrorCompany.com
Facebook.com/sinisterhorrorcompany
Twitter @SinisterHC

Lightning Source UK Ltd.
Milton Keynes UK
UKOW01f1551241116
PP1561300001B/1/P